WHITE SQUAW

#21:

ARIZONA LAYDOWN
E.J. HUNTER

ZEBRA BOOKS
KENSINGTON PUBLISHING CORP.

Chapter 1

She stood at the edge of the woodland, a lone figure, wind-whipped, alternately concealed and brought into bold relief by the streamers of thick fog. A weak, dying sun provided no warmth. Up-slope, among the trees, something stirred. Her gaze darted toward the movement. Ominous foreboding sent chills along her spine. She reached instinctively for the big Colt Bisley that should be strapped to her side. It wasn't there! The flicker between lower branches of the ancient pines and firs grew more distinct, resolved into the figure of a man, silhouetted by the lowering orange ball behind him. Suddenly she wanted to run, to seek comfort and safety elsewhere.

Desperation shattered her control when she tried to turn and could not. The dark figure came closer. She felt like an insect trapped in a teardrop of amber as the mist swirled around her unmoving legs. The air turned apricot as puffs of dust rose around high black boots and the faceless being increased his pace to a lope. The black leather duster, worn like a cape, flapped like demon wings as the menacing form spread wide his arms. Only a few feet separated them when a piercing shaft of infernal light illuminated his face.

Rebecca Caldwell recognized the terrible visage of Chris Starret in that dazzling brightness, and she

5

screamed. Cruel mouth spread wide in a ghastly grimace, Chris Starret revealed long, needle-pointed canine teeth and, protruding from his forehead, a pair of satanic horns. Rendered numb and helpless, Rebecca Caldwell screamed again.

And jolted awake, to find herself secure in the Denver rooming house bed of Gaylen Stanton. Her long black hair in disarray, she looked at her surroundings with wide, frightened eyes of dark blue. Gaylen lay there beside her, lost in the deep sleep induced by long and satisfying lovemaking. Only a dream. No, a nightmare. Rebecca shivered and hugged her knees to her chest like a small child. Her full, sensuous lips stretched into a hard line. Gaylen stirred, prodded from his well of slumber by her cry of alarm.

"Wha—what is it?" he mumbled.

"Nothing—uh—I," Rebecca muttered defensively. "Oh, it was a bad dream. Nothing, really."

Gaylen sat up, put a protective arm around Rebecca's shoulders. "Tell me about it, Becky."

In short, painful spurts, Rebecca described the rapidly fleeing images from her nightmare. Gaylen consoled and calmed her, nodding, cooing words of understanding and concern. Slowly the terror and tension left her. Gaylen's soothing strokes became more intense, ardent. Rebecca sensed the subtle change and responded to it out of sudden, burning need. She turned slightly so she could hug Gaylen.

They clung in silence while the Regulator clock ticked on the wall. From far off came the faint bugle of a premature rooster. Gaylen's big, firm hands traced spirals on Rebecca's bare back. Their breathing roughened and they kissed. A shiver of anticipation cast away Rebecca's fright as she probed Gaylen's warm, sweet mouth with her tongue. With one hand she sought his hot, rigid organ and began a gentle stroking.

"Aaah, that's nice," Gaylen gasped, breaking their embrace.

6

"Oh, Gaylen, Gaylen, I love to be loving with you. I need you oooh, sooo badly," Rebecca moaned.

"Hush, now, hush. It will all go away. Chris Starret is dead and buried in that mine in Wyoming. Just love me. Just—come here and love me," he gently demanded, as he tugged her into the shelter of his strength.

Fingers that had held a smoking revolver, a knife, and a Sioux tomahawk pressed against Gaylen's chest, nudging him into a supine position, his back against the welcome coolness of a muslin sheet. With lithe assurance, Rebecca raised one silken leg and straddled Gaylen's middle. She thrilled to the touch of his hand on her thigh. Languidly Gaylen slid his fingers upward until the tips made contact with the sparce, raven strands that covered her heated mound. His restraint fled as he reached her pulsing cleft and found it wet and ready.

Rebecca trembled with delight as she guided his long, fat member to the cloven portal of her womanhood. Excitedly she introduced the sensitive bulb to the leafy fronds within, and they parted welcomingly to accept his pleasant penetration. Rebecca bit at her lower lip and lowered herself in a rush, consuming half of the gift so joyfully offered her. The sudden, expanding presence wrung a gasp from deep in her soul. Her heart pounded and she groaned as the latent power filled her.

A tiny shriek burst from her full, sensual lips as she lunged downward and took Gaylen to her depths. A passion-born shudder caused her firm, globular breasts to sway, and her shiny black braids swayed with the rhythm she set up driving Gaylen's throbbing shaft back and forth. Shuddering, she began to grind her pubic mound against his pelvic arch, releasing dizzying waves of euphoria for both of them. Rebecca's hips churned and Gaylen undulated his groin to match her fervor.

Her azure eyes wide, Rebecca began to grunt and moan as her jabs increased with the frenzy of her desire. She leaned forward, rigid nipples brushing Gaylen's bare chest. He captured her in his arms and held on tight as

7

the first faint warning of approaching eruption cramped his belly. Rocking on the sea of Eros, their fragile human emotions were adrift in a maelstrom of towering waves of intense glory.

"Oooh, Len—Len—ooooh, Gaaaaylennnn!" Rebecca wailed as she underwent a magnificent climax. Her churning consumption of his maleness faltered a moment as the throes of her completion gripped her, then resumed with new vigor.

Accompanied by the creak and groan of the hard-used bed, the ecstatic pair strove to their utmost toward a mutual consummation of their bliss. Caught in the stream, they bucked and plunged until the cataract loomed close. Divine madness seized Gaylen, and he threw more violent force into his hammer-blow thrusts.

"Becky—Becky—Becky-Becky-Becky!" Gaylen chanted as he rose to the ultimate conclusion.

Then it happened and a sweet, velvety blackness washed over them as their amorous combat ended, as always, in mutual victory and defeat. Sighs and coos replaced the more strident notes of earlier expression. All terrors had been banished, yet even while the warm glow of nectarous climax slowly faded, Rebecca could not help but believe that the dissipated horrors of her dream had been some sort of ominous premonition.

From east to west in the northern quarter of Arizona Territory, the land had long been disputed between the warlike Utes and the more peaceful Shoshone from the region of the Green River. Now they both shared in contesting the white man over the same territory. It had taken a century of negotiations between the tribes to allow the Shoshone hunting rights in the mountainous country at the extreme southern part of their domain. Now the Shoshone in particular found the pressure of increasing white population a matter of great concern. A delegation led by Walks Around, graying principal civil

8

chief of the southern Shoshone, came to the new white settlement of Flagstaff in Arizona Territory.

They were met and welcomed by Lieutenant Colonel Jeremy Alford, who commanded the northern district of the Department of Arizona, under command of General George B. Crook. In deference to his guests, Lieutenant Colonel Alford suggested the meeting be held in a pine-shaded glade outside the small military outpost on the edge of town. Warblers and woodpeckers made cheerful noise as the chiefs arranged themselves on bison robes in a circle in which Walks Around and Jeremy Alford sat side-by-side.

"More white men come every moon," Walks Around began after the amenities had been observed. "They go into places that are not theirs."

"Arizona Territory is a part of the United States now," Alford reminded through an interpreter. "White men can come and go as they please."

Walks Around grunted his disappointment. "Not so. There are marks on paper, a—ah, treaty that gives the land from here to beyond the big canyon to the Indians. The Utes and our own people alike share in this. It is not for the white man to go there."

Alford underwent momentary discomfort. "That—ah—may be so. But it is not reservation land. There are no provisions to police it."

"It is our hunting ground," Walks Around snapped. "It's not for the white man. Why do you let them come to where they are not supposed to be?"

"I—ah—don't 'let' them, Walks Around. They—ah—just come."

"Then stop them."

"It's not that easy, Chief Walks Around. I lack the men to enforce the treaty."

"Why is that?" Walks Around demanded.

"Half of my command has been ordered south to aid General Crook against the Apache, and the rest are already in the field, to keep watch on the Piute and the

9

Navaho. That leaves only a small complement here at Flagstaff."

Walks Around exchanged glances with his fellow chiefs. "The Apache come and go as they wish, white men do not steal their hunting grounds. Why should we be different?"

Alford quirked one corner of his wide, generous mouth. "General Crook is in the process of ending all of that for the Apache. Soon they, too, will live on reservations like your people, watched over by soldiers."

Anger clouded Walks Around's brow. "We are not children that we need watching over. The White Father in Wash-ing-ton says this when he makes the treaty to allow us to hunt in this country like free men. Now other white men try to take that away. The marks on paper say that you must protect us, like you protect the white men. That is all we ask."

Alford studied the implacable faces in the circle. Not a one had spoken. Obviously a consensus had been reached before they journeyed to Flagstaff. Lieutenant Colonel Alford worked his pursed lips in and out, brow furrowed in concentration. At last he sighed and met Walks Around's eyes with reluctance.

"We are sorely limited in manpower. All the same, we'll do what we can. That I promise you. I will personally do all I can to help."

Big Mac Kellogg stood on the steep slope, fists on hips, below a bulge of big, yet hard and fat-free belly. His gray-green eyes twinkled with the sun as he examined the seemingly endless sea of fir, pine, cedar, and a host of hardwoods. They could cut for eternity here, or so it seemed. A cool, gentle breeze ruffled his thick, sandy hair. He let it grow wild, a tendency to curl accenting its bushy nature. Big Mac more than liked what he saw. His huge, muscular body fairly quivered with excitement over the prospects this vista offered.

10

Here was a land rich in gold, silver, copper, and most of all, timber. With bison-grazed, treeless plains to the east, and desert to the south and west, nearly half the nation cried for lumber. A free-wheeling logging operation like this one could do very well. During the past week the last of a long stream of cruisers, fallers, sawyers, and log wranglers arrived in town. Now Big Mac thrilled to the ring of cruising axes, marking the southern boundary of the open public land he had chosen to make his fortune. The government, far off in Washington on the Potomac, would never be aware of who denuded the publicly owned forest.

Fully aware of the army's helplessness, greedy white entrepreneurs had been quick to set up schemes to rape the land. Why should he be left out? He was part of the people, the public, wasn't he? Big Mac had it figured that way and saw no reason some Eastern sharper should benefit while he hesitated to seize the main chance. Only one flaw marred his plan, Big Mac acknowledged.

Already the mountains swarmed with gold-seekers. Prospectors filed their claims in droves and jealously guarded everything on their piece of land. Big Mac wanted them out of what he saw as *his* claim. To facilitate that he had hired a dozen deadly, feral gunhawks. He looked on the breed with contempt and disdain, but he treated them fairly and received loyal, valuable service in return. To ride herd on them, he had engaged the services of a man whose reputation would keep the men in line.

What Big Mac Kellogg didn't know was that Chris Starret had brought along twenty-five men of his own choosing, whom he kept out of sight until the time was right. Meanwhile, Starret, along with his right-hand man, John Blackjack Duffey, and Kellogg's chief enforcer, Bull Grayson, conducted the business designated by their employer.

Five silent, hard-faced men swung down from their

11

mounts. The burbling music of the mountain stream masked the sound of their approach and dismounting. A constant banter between partners, who had been old friends long before their prospecting venture, had also distracted them from hearing the visitors arrive. One of the gold-seekers paused in his endless effort of shoveling loads of creek bottom into the riffle box to mop his brow. In the process he looked up at the sloping bank and saw the new arrivals.

"Howdy, fellers. What brings you out our way?" he asked genially.

"Why, we came to make you an offer you'll not regret," Blackjack Duffey stated with grim humor. "Matter of fact, you'll just up an' die if you don't say yes."

Suspicion clouded the prospector's eyes. "Don't reckon I know what you're gettin' at. Speak plain."

Blackjack fished inside his white linen duster and drew out a folded document with a blue legal cover. "You're gonna sell your claim to me," he informed the partners in a growl.

"We ain't sellin' to anybody," the second prospector snapped.

"That's right," his partner affirmed.

Blackjack shrugged and produced a weary expression. With a nod, he passed his associates a meaningful gaze. At once they started forward. The prospectors took steps backward, the one holding his shovel like a rifle at port arms.

"Get 'em," one of the toughs snarled.

Moving like a single being, the four hardcases lunged at the frightened, uncertain prospectors. One retreated again, splashing in the clear, cold water. His boot heel came down on a smooth, round rock and he sprawled backward, laying full out in the stream. A cry of alarm rang briefly from his lips before the two enforcers grabbed him and shoved his head under. His partner uttered a bark of anger and took a swipe with his shovel.

It rang musically when it struck the side of a hardcase's head. "Aaaagh! Goddam, he done hit me," one bully boy bleated, eyes unfocused and an ear bleeding.

Blackjack Duffey remained on dry ground, arms folded over his chest, an amused quirk to his full, petulant lips. Spluttering and howling, the first prospector had his head yanked out of the water. Noisily he sucked in air for a brief span before the men holding him plunged him below the surface again. Duffey tapped the toe of one highly polished, narrow, pointed boot as though keeping time to unheard music. Once more the pair of thugs tried to take the shovel-wielding partner.

This time they ducked at the appropriate time and the deadly implement went wide, follow-through carrying it far to the left of its owner. Rendered thusly vulnerable, both enforcers charged him. He wisely dropped the improvised weapon and went at them with fists.

Knuckles smacked and thudded against bare and padded flesh as the hardcases uttered ferocious roars and waded in to their opponent. With vicious jabs and hooks, and a well-placed kick between his legs, they worried the prospector to his knees. Then they plunged him into the water like his partner.

Alternately the partners rose and descended, gasping, choking, begging for mercy. None came. At a curt jerk of Blackjack's head, the enforcers dragged their half-drowned victims onto the bank. Duffey bent low, smiling, his face only inches from theirs.

"Well now, when you dry off a mite, you'll be ready to sign."

"You can go to hell," the spunky prospector growled.

"What's that? Sure you don't think we're going to all this trouble and you not getting paid? Is that it? Well, my friends, you'll be rewarded quite handsomely for your claim. A thousand dollars. Think of it. Five hundred apiece."

"Hell, we can make that much in a month with that riffle box," the outspoken one spat.

13

"Only if you're alive, bucko." Duffey rose and flicked his index finger in a commanding gesture.

Immediately the four toughs began to kick the sodden men. Grunts of effort blended with the muffled groans of protest. Then the smaller prospector cried out at the splintering sound of breaking teeth.

Buck Rainey stood over him, his carbine held ready for another butt-stroke. John Duffey raised a hand to restrain him. "No. We need them in shape to sign the papers." To the battered prospectors, "Are you ready to sign now? You'll still be paid a handsome amount."

"A-all right. Ain't worth dyin' and gettin' nothin' for it," one agreed.

Duffey produced the papers, then fumbled in his saddlebag for a screw-top inkwell and steel-nib pen. Shakily the defeated men signed at the indicated places. Then Duffey produced a thick sheaf of bills and handed them over.

"That's a thousand dollars." With a short gesture he indicated that the other hardcases should mount up. "Y'all head back. I want to convince these fellows not to complain about the way they sold their claim."

Duffey talked slowly and softly to the downcast prospectors until he figured Kellogg's men had ridden far enough to be uncertain as to the direction from which a sound might come. Then he rose from his squatting position and walked to his horse.

"Well, time to go," he announced offhandedly as he slid his .45 Colt from its holster.

Whistling tunelessly, Duffey turned and shot both of the prospectors in the head. Then he stepped over to them and removed the money from their corpses. Still whistling, he mounted and rode off.

Chapter 2

A donkey's impudent bray came from the direction of the livery stable. The shouts and laughter of children at play came through the thin walls of unpainted boards on the edge of Flagstaff, Arizona Territory. A large, unprofessionaly painted sign in black block letters announced it: SALES OFFICE & KELLOGG LUMBER COMPANY. Inside furnishings reflected the same indifference to refinements.

In the forward portion of the single room a flat desk for laying out building plans, three straight-back chairs, and a spittoon constituted the only amenities. Beyond a low, fencelike barrier with dual swinging gates, a hat rack, potbellied stove, cold now in late summer, and a rolltop desk completed the decor. Seated at the rolltop, Chris Starret looked approvingly at John Duffey.

"So we're a thousand richer, and Kellogg's got the trees on that claim. This is penny-ante stuff, Chris. When do we get to the real money?"

"Soon, John, real soon," Chris promised.

He studied Blackjack Duffey's hard and disapproving face and let his gaze stray to the close-cropped, curly black hair. When they had first met, as members of the Plummer Gang, there hadn't been streaks of gray in Duffey's Black Irish locks. At only thirty-seven, Duffey shouldn't have any now, Chris considered. He worried too much. Duffey's murky, odd-colored eyes had an unusual brightness that could be warning of near-madness. In deference to that, Chris decided to confide more than he usually did to an underling.

"We start selling lumber in Phoenix soon. Then the money will start to flow. There'll be plenty opportunity to skim a lot off that. Big Mac's got his fallers cutting trees, and the sawmill will be completed soon. When the land's stripped of trees, we'll be able to buy cheap and sell dear to flood of pilgrims that'll be headed this way to start a new life."

Duffey kept his eyes fixed on the steel-gray gaze of the man across from him. Chris ran a hand lightly over his bald pate and pursed full lips. He noticed Duffey's impatient posture and spoke again.

"You wanted to say something? Do it."

"Big business it might be," Duffey complained. "I'm used to scooping twenty or thirty thousand out of a bank and going off to enjoy life for a while. When do we see that kind of money?"

Chris gave him a pitying smile. "We play our cards right and 'that kind of money' will be pocket change. Big Mac doesn't give a damn about mineral rights or the ground itself. I do. He'll wipe out the forest, make a quick killing in lumber sales, and move on to strip another piece of country. We'll stay and hold onto all rights, even water. Also," he added with an irrepressible grin, "what's to say that once Big Mac puts his profits into the local banks, they can't be robbed?"

Duffey beamed. "I like that. Oh, I do like that."

She couldn't keep away from it. The site fascinated her. Fighting that part of her which cried out to her to stay away, Rebecca Caldwell slowly advanced to the lip of the collapsed mine. It remained exactly as she had last seen it. Every detail had been etched into memory on that violent, conclusive day when the outlaw marauders had

16

been vanquished by the Arapaho and Shoshone, allied for the first time in history. Against all reason, Rebecca knelt and leaned out over the aged shaft.

Deep down there, Chris Starret lay under a mound of debris, buried for all time. She leaned further. It had to be a quirk of the light that penetrated the old mine. A faint red glow appeared at the center of the mound of dirt, rock, and timber. While she watched and gauged it, it intensified in brightness. Rebecca tried to push away from the edge, to escape down the mountain side, but she could not.

With the fierce thunderclap of an explosion, the litter at the bottom of the mine burst upward. Through it rose a huge human figure, arms wide-spread. His motion effortlessly brushed aside mounds of dirt, heavy rocks and large shoring beams. Backlighted by the awful glow of hell-fire, his face could still be discerned as that of Chris Starret. His mouth opened, twisted into a bellow of rage, and along with him he brought a host of demons. Rebecca Caldwell screamed and fought invisible bonds in an effort to flee.

Chris Starret came closer and she screamed again. "Becky! What is it?" Gaylen Stanton cried, alarmed and jolted out of sound sleep.

Rebecca Caldwell stared sightlessly at the opposite wall. "I . . . saw him. It—it happened again. The nightmare. This time it was at the mine. Chris Starret rose right out of the bowels of hell."

"Oh, Becky, Becky, that's not reasonable. It can't happen."

Big, frightened blue eyes turned on him. "Oh, yes. Yes, it can. I saw it, I . . ." She shuddered and choked back a sob, then visibly wrestled control over her frayed emotions. "No. You're right. It was—was only a nightmare."

Gaylen eyed her warily. "Perhaps . . . I mean, maybe you should see a doctor about this. Sometimes the oddest things bring on bad dreams. A bit of potato, some spoiled

17

beef, a blot of mustard," Gaylen babbled on, unconsciously quoting Charles Dickens.

"No," Rebecca responded a bit too quickly. "I—er, I mean I don't think a conventional doctor would be able to do anything for me. Wh—what I'm experiencing is more like the vision images of a Sioux warrior, or a medicine man's dream. It's not . . . madness."

Taken aback, Gaylen could only dissemble. "There are no Sioux to interpret it for you around Denver."

Rebecca caught a subtle nuance in Gaylen's tone. "Don't patronize me. And don't talk down about Spirit Dreams," she snapped, a small, white-hot anger coloring her words. "They are as real to any Sioux, real to me as the Spirit World itself, or the Great Spirit himself. What I need to do is get purified and talk with a medicine man."

Unsuspected by either of them, Gaylen's childhood roots in Christian abhorrence of "witchcraft" rose from the depths of memory to combine with a heretofore unexpressed prejudice against Indians—not an uncommon combination on the frontier or the western part of the nation.

"Well then, that's settled," Gaylen blurted nastily. "There's certainly no witch-doctor for you to run off to."

Reacting to what might be called an emotional slap in the face, Rebecca curbed her own quick-to-flare temper. "No," she agreed in a sweet voice that should have been a warning in itself. "But there is an Arapaho reservation nearby, with at least one medicine man, and I intend to go there."

Still drugged with sleep and bountiful sex, Gaylen burst out in howls of scornful laughter. "Yo-you're a civilized . . . wo-woman, for Pete's sake," he guffawed.

Sadly, it looked to Rebecca like the romance was over. Vaguely her mind dredged up little snippets of conversation which she had at the time suppressed. *"Those people,"* Gaylen had said on several occasions. *"Their kind."* She now recalled how his nose had wrinkled at the odors of the Arapaho camp. Unwanted memory supplied

18

how Gaylen had shied from a comradely embrace with Shining Horse. In spite of the hour, her father's blood directed her.

"Hey—hey, what are you doing?" Gaylen demanded as Rebecca climbed from the bed and went to the large oak armoire where her clothes hung.

"I'm leaving. I need to find out the meaning of these dreams and I don't need to be laughed at for wanting to. I'll move to a hotel, then contact the Arapaho village."

"In the middle of the night?" Gaylen demanded, uncertain.

"They're open all night," Rebecca cooly reminded him.

"You're not . . ." Gaylen blurted, mentally reviewing their conversation. "You're not taking offense at what—what I said?"

"Why shouldn't I?" Rebecca demanded, loosing her anger as she stuffed clothing into two valises. "For five years of my life, from fourteen to nineteen, I lived as a Sioux woman, I married and bore a child to a Sioux man. My father was a war chief of the *Tiśayaota,* the Red Top Lodge band. Why should I not be offended? What seems to you uproariously funny, I take quite seriously. I'm sorry, Gaylen, I truly am. At least part of me is. The other part isn't the least sorry. I'll find out what this is all about and then . . . then I just might come back. You've been good to me and for me, and at times wonderfully sweet. But I must know, I must find out. Good-bye, Gaylen."

"I can't let you . . . I can't . . ." Gaylen began to protest, though by then she was out the door.

Even the casual observer knew at once that Christopher Allen Starret had been born to wear fine clothes, smoke expensive cigars, and drink champagne. His patrician profile made ladies' knees weak. His sole drawback was the fact that he was entirely bald. Not by nature's attrition, but by request. Upon his arrival in Phoenix, Arizona Territory, his first undertaking had been to seek out a discreet barber, whom he paid handsomely to shave his pate. Then he settled in at the Hohokam, the luxury hotel built of native tufa rock, like the Maricopa County courthouse and jail. After that he made a call on the local newspapers and placed flamboyant notices informing the populace that a representative of Kellogg Lumber was in town and selling all manner of boards, planks, rafters, and beams, suitable for construction. Then he found himself a trollop and retired to his suite on the third floor of the Hohokam.

"You're a pretty little thing," he murmured to the soiled dove as he removed his coat and vest.

She actually blushed, which increased Chris' appreciation and ardor. Small, most likely not even legally old enough to be in a saloon, the girl had big, glowing black eyes, a heart-shaped face, and a slight stature that gave her a childlike appearance. A recent initiate to the Calling of Venus, she didn't know exactly how to deal with someone who wanted to engage her charms for an entire night. Particularly one obviously too sober to fall off into numb slumber after the first go-around. The pink tint to her peaches-and-cream cheeks grew toward scarlet as she fumbled with the tricky buttons of her scanty costume.

"Allow me," Chris offered suavely.

He had her unhooked to the base of her spine in a flicker of time. Smiling he walked around her, inspecting her enticingly curved back in the manner of a buyer judging livestock. Caught in his intense gaze, the girl suddenly became nervous.

"I—ah—don't know if . . . what I mean is, what do you like? How do you want to do it?"

His big, long-fingered hands spanning her narrow waist, which dislodged her dress and let it fall forward, Chris lifted her lightly off the floor, a huge smile spreading his full lips. "I like it . . . every way there is to have it, my pigeon. In every opening, in every position, standing or lying down, or in a porch swing." He bent low

20

and took a virginal nipple in his mouth.

"Oh!" It came out a surprised little squeak.

The rough, rugged types around Phoenix had little in the way of finesse. Few, if any, appreciated a woman's sensibilities. Horror tales from her childhood, told by mother, grandmother, and a host of aunts, of how a woman must suffer this unwanted and unpleasant attention from men, surged into her consciousness. Now, in stark contrast, she found herself terribly excited by the prospect. Her head swam and she had a great hollowness in her belly. Her heart pounded and her breath came in short gasps. Nimbly she began to unbutton this wonderful man's shirt. Only one thing bothered her. Why hadn't he taken off his hat?

She quickly forgot it when she encountered the ample, stiffened evidence of his own arousal, tightly pressed against the double layer of cloth over her moistening cleft. Delightedly she wriggled herself against his member. Oh, this—this is what is should always be like, she thrilled . . . what, for all the tales of pain and nastiness, she had always dreamed it could be.

At an early age she had discovered that her puffy little mound was the source of indescribable pleasure. She need only touch it, rub it a little, insert a finger, then two, and how quickly it got wet and slick. Then, when she grew closer to her teens, other objects, long, fat, and smooth, brought explosions of even more exquisite enjoyment. Let her aunts, her mother, let them all gabble about how degrading it was. She knew better.

"Umm, you're an eager little bitch," Chris murmured, nuzzling the base of her throat.

"Uh-huh," she said in a daze of euphoria. "We're gonna have sooo much fun."

Swiftly, before she realized it, they lay naked on the bed. She held his large, silken manhood in both hands, squeezed and stroked it, pulled it toward her hotly awaiting entry, and moaned with desire. He squeezed and pinched, licked and kissed her breasts. One hand slid up

21

and down her inner thighs. then she had him where she wanted him, and she slathered the fat bulb of his throbbing phallus in the ample wetness that surged from her. When he pierced her all the July Fourth celebrations of her childhood erupted at once.

While he thrust deep and fully into her, she faded away into an oblivion of rapture, with only one tiny thought a niggling reminder of the real world. They had somehow gotten out of all their clothes, removed footwear, and fallen into the comfort of the big bed, and yet . . . and yet, he still wore his hat.

"Yes, sir, you can't go wrong with this lumber, I guarantee," Chris Starret said expansively. "Trees are coming down in droves. There's a kiln for drying and seasoning lumber, and a big sawmill. Actually, you're getting a head start on your competition if you act now. Big Mac heard about the building boom in Phoenix and sent me down here to help out. A lot of what's being cut now should have gone to Flagstaff, but you boys seemed to be in greater need." He gave a sly wink and fingered the gold chain that spanned his flat abdomen from one vest pocket to the other.

Clothes indeed must make the man, for no one had seen the feral gunslinger behind the soft gray wool with discreet pinstripes. This was the third caller that morning and Starret had taken deposits from both of the others. Over a hundred thousand board feet of lumber sold. Not bad for the first day of operation. It began to reach Chris that a great deal more money could be made in Big Mac's operation then he had expected. Particularly when you sold the same consignments of lumber over again three or four times. Reflecting on it, Chris flashed a salesman's smile at his latest customer and rubbed his palms together.

"There's nothing like being first," Chris confided. "Of course, it will take some while to get that much lumber

22

down here to Phoenix by wagon. One of the things we're working on is to get the Southern Pacific to run a spur up to Flagstaff from their Texas and Pacific Southern Trail route." Chris gave a nod toward the door and lowered his voice in a conspiratorial manner. "I feel certain there may be some among our lucky first customers who have the perception and the wherewithal to take advantage of such advance news and, ah, invest wisely."

Eyes alight with avarice, the portly gentleman wanted fifty thousand board feet of seasoned lumber to construct a three-story hotel with a first floor and corner facings of native tufa stone. "Are you implying that if I buy my lumber exclusively from your firm, you might cut me in on the spur development?"

Gotcha! Chris rejoiced at his acumen in evaluating his fellow men. He replied solely with a grave nod. The more mysterious and shady a deal appeared, the faster the greedy would jump in. The fact that the railroad spur investment company existed only in his imagination only whetted Chris' eagerness to sell shares to the suckers. A prime one sat across from him now, the way he saw it. Time to let it soak in and fester a little.

"Now, for the breakdown on your order. How much hardwood, fir, cedar?"

For the rest of the day Chris did remarkable business. He planted the seed of his con with four others, all anxious to be "on the inside" of any railroad development. He would be here three more days. If all went well, he would leave Phoenix a multi-millionaire.

By the time he made ready to return to Flagstaff, the number and dollar size of the deposit checks had grown to the point of temptation. Over four hundred thousand. Real money, which he wouldn't have to spend a long time cultivating out of the marks he had set up in the railroad scheme. He could simply take it and move on. San Francisco sounded nice this time of the year. Perhaps he should look into it. His larcenous heart beat faster at the prospect.

Then, when five of Big Mac's gunhands showed up headed by Bull Grayson, his ambition beat slower. He and John Duffey weren't quite good enough to handle that much opposition, Chris acknowledged. Particularly when it came to explaining a shoot-out to the law.

"You done real good," the huge, barrel-like Grayson growled when informed of the total deposits. "Mr. Kellogg will be right pleased."

"These suckers are going to have a long wait to get any of that lumber I sold," Chris observed cheerfully.

"Not necessarily. That deposit money is for buying more lumbermill equipment. We'll freight it from here to Flagstaff."

"Still, I've sold what lumber we can produce four and five times over," Chris informed the beetle-browed enforcer. "That's a damn good profit, considering only one customer is going to get each parcel."

"Nope. They're all going to get what they ordered." Grayson towered over Chris, at three inches over six feet, his crooked nose, broken many times in brawls, like a damaged plowshare on his wide, flat face. "Big Mac don't mind selling lumber more than once, and making people wait on delivery, but takin' folks' money and not providin' for them at all he considers dishonest. We'll be relievin' you of those deposits so's we can buy the donkey engine and other stuff Big Mac wants."

Chris complied with ill grace, his mind already working on refinements to his railroad spur con. Somehow, he promised himself, he would turn this around and come out on top. Anyone as honest as Big Mac Kellogg deserved to be taken for a bundle.

Chapter 3

Birds twittered in the huge, ancient conifers that dotted a mountainside some thirty miles northwest of Denver, Colorado. Below the reaching branches, in a sheltered glade, a thin whisp of pale white smoke rose from the small hole in a brush arbor. High and thin, the singing voice of a man issued from it.

"*Hu—na ha! Hey—yah ha! San—teeyah ha!*" The squat, wheezened Arapaho paused, his lined face taking on a gullied expression of kindness. "Take this, drink of it. Then I will join you," Bent Horn instructed.

Rebecca Caldwell, naked except for a soft, well-cured sash of beaded elkhide around her waist, accepted the bison horn cup and took a long pull of its contents. The concoction of roots, herbs, and pulped peyote buttons had a bitter, acrid flavor that left a chalky coating on her tongue. It also numbed the tissues of her mouth and throat. She blinked lazily and watched the medicine man sip from the same cup.

Sighing in contented anticipation, Bent Horn set the cup aside and sprinkled a mixture of herbs and pine needles on the coals of the small fire between them. Then he lifted the braided horsetail hair rope that was fastened to a copper ring at the center front of Rebecca's sash.

"This is so you will not get away from me and wander forever in the Spirit World," he told her with a chuckle.

Rebecca started to smile, sharing the small joke. Abruptly the scene before her shifted, canted to one side and became blurry. She felt the beginning of a stomach cramp as she squinted to try and keep the medicine man in focus. Her eyes closed with languid, hypnotic slowness.

She opened them to a black sphere studded with familiar constellations. Except for now the known had become alien in their closeness. Turning, she saw her bare, tawny body far away below her position in the sphere. It looked tiny, doll-like. Bent Horn sat there, hunched over, one hand clutching the horse hair cord. He twitched it and she felt the tug.

Obediently she turned away from the odd human creatures below. A gnarled coppery hand, glowing with an eerie phosphorescence, pointed her along the path. Rebecca began to walk. The ebon velvet globe expanded, split like an opening fruit. Brightness showed through. A huge figure came into the range of her vision. The tall, barrel-chested Indian male, his features obscured by a hazy mist, bent low and spoke to her.

"You are White Robe Woman, of the *Tisayaota Oglalahca*. You have come with a burden. Here, sit beside me and tell me of your vision that disturbs."

Patiently, with the obedience and small voice of a child, Rebecca related all that she recalled of her nightmares. The lordly Spirit figure nodded sympathetically. When she completed the recitation, he reached toward her and she felt the tingle of an unearthly touch.

"Go now," the celestial voice instructed her. "Here is Bent Horn, who will take you to Earth Mother. She will show you signs by which you can interpret your dream."

The pastoral scene melted and dissolved as Rebecca felt a tug on the binding cord and saw Bent Horn at her side. Everything disappeared in a whirl as Rebecca and her guide spun through the Spirit World to the place of Earth Mother.

A heartrendingly sweet feminine voice spoke out of the vast reaches of the Land of All Summer. "You will see these signs and remember them when you return to that mud ball where man dwells," the kindly Spirit told her.

Insubstantial, like transparent clouds, objects rose out of the ethereal expanse of golden, tall grass prairie. A white bunny, hardly old enough to be away from its mother, hopped toward her. Tawny and sleek, a cougar stalked the white rabbit. Hovering in the shimmering air above the cougar Rebecca saw an item at first unrecognizable. Then she realized it was an Indian's interpretation of a white man's book. It emitted a terrible odor of death and decay. A hank of thick, blond hair hung from its pages. Suddenly she gasped and shrank back as a figure galloped toward her on a white horse. It had the face of Chris Starret. Fluttering on a bush in the wind of Starret's passage she saw a man's red shirt.

In the next instant, as Rebecca tried to burn the images into memory, the scene dimmed, swirled, and spun madly. A ghostly, interstellar wind howled in her ears. She tried to cry out, but could not, felt the hearty tug on her tether, and awakened back in the brush Spirit lodge.

Bent Horn smiled at her. "You have had a successful journey, Daughter of the Dakota. The man on the white horse tells us that your dreams were truly Spirit messages. The one called Chris Starret did indeed survive his fall into the mine and is at his evil work again."

"Then I must go after him," Rebecca said with a thick tongue.

"Do not go, my child, until you hear the rest." Bent Horn paused and took a long swallow of water, then passed the gourd dipper to Rebecca. "Before you can confront Starret, you will encounter the cougar. He may be in Spirit form or very real. A yellow-haired white eye and the book figure into the story of the cougar. The white rabbit is young. When you learn of him, he will have a lot to do with the difficulty of your task. The *oglésa*—the red shirt, in your Lakota tongue—will be

27

important in how you solve the problem of Starret. All these things you must carry with you."

"Where is he? Where do I find Starret?" Rebecca demanded, impatience overcoming the languor of her drug-induced state.

"You must go into the land where the sun goes to sleep to stop him," Bent Horn told her. "There is . . . nothing more I can tell you."

Rebecca started to rise. "You have told me enough, Bent Horn."

"Timmmm-berrrrr!"

The faller's chilling cry echoed through the woods as another giant splintered on its thin pivot and came crashing to the ground at Big Mac Kellogg's cutting camp.

"Timmmm-berrrr!" followed before the reverberations ended.

Another monument to antiquity tottered and descended into a cloud of dust and flying pine needles. All around, trees came down one after another, sometimes as many as three at a time.

"Fire in the hole!" a powder man bellowed.

A deep *whump* that could be faintly heard in distant Flagstaff sounded from the mountainside, and then the ground heaved; ripples were felt half a mile away. Gouts of dirt and granite mushroomed out of the face of the raw cut in the slope. More trees crackled and gave up their lives.

"Goddamn good job," Big Mac rumbled, fists on ample hips as he surveyed his new kingdom. "Keep it up, boys."

"We're fellin' a hundred trees a day, Mac," one foreman announced.

"That's good. Log 'em out and put 'em on the skids. We've got two bucksaws and a plainer and joiner operatin' now. When the new equipment gets here we can really fly."

Big Mac departed from the front lines of his war on nature to return to his lumbering operation further down the mountain. He failed to notice three dark copper faces, each reflecting muted anger and confusion.

Seated on the saddle pads of their hunting ponies, the Shoshone braves looked with wonder and perplexity at the antics of the white-eyes. They accepted that all whites acted in an unreasonable manner. But to harvest trees too big to use as lodge poles and too difficult to render into firewood made no sense. Why did they do this? And the thunder sound worried them. Did the white men have their own golden "shoots-long-way" guns with them? What made the mountain vomit up its very being?

"These are strange things," Victor Cuts Hair remarked quietly to his companions.

"That is true," Burning Ridge agreed. "If the white-eyes go on like this, our southern hunting grounds will be no more and the land will be scarred forever."

"Fires take all the trees and the Earth Mother brings back life," Fox Killer reminded his friends.

"I have seen that," Burning Ridge agreed. "But I have also seen what happens when the white-eyes take the trees and do not burn off the brush. The land turns bare and will not grow anything. We must take this to the council."

Walks Around cautioned peace, as the young men knew he would. He would not bend on the issue of taking the warpath against the men who despoiled the land. He did agree to send a deputation to the white-eyes who cut down the trees, asking them to spare some so the forest would regrow and the land not die. Burning Ridge and Fox Killer went along.

"See what the white-eyes do?" Burning Ridge said angrily to the older members of the delegation.

He waved his arm to encompass the denuded acres of mountain side where magnificent evergreens, centuries old, once grew. Only branches and bare ground remained. A touch of sadness entered the expressions of all who had come.

"We'll ride to the camp of the white-eye destroyers," Elk Tooth announced.

"It is this way," Fox Killer directed, reining his pony to the south.

They found the camp in a bustle of activity. Men went about with boards on their shoulders, while carpenters labored to construct more barracks and storage sheds. Hammers tapped and saws rasped the afternoon air. Here and there large columns of smoke rose as the waste from trimming logs burned. This brought further scowls from the Shoshone visitors. A hundred yards from the camp, one of the loggers slicking out a fat-based fir looked up and saw their approach.

"Hey," he bellowed. "We got Injuns comin'."

Others picked up the call and the entire worksite grew silent. Loggers and cruisers, clutching axes, carpenters and cooks, and the sawyers from small mill at the camp came forward, forming a large semicircle around the Shoshone.

"What do you want here, Injun?" a burly man demanded.

"We come to talk of the trees," Burning Ridge said in his stiff English. "To take them all is a bad thing. You must listen to us, we do not want trouble between your people and ours. Only that you cut down trees with care. Go among them. Take the best for what you need, one in each three. Leave the others to grow and make the land well again."

"Are you kidding?" a foreman guffawed. "Only one third of what's here? Nobody's crazy enough to do that."

"Yeah, Charlie's right," another joined in. "That don't make sense, Injun."

"Why do you take the trees?" Burning Ridge demanded.

"Why, to make houses for folks to live in, build stores

30

and barns."

"More whites come into our land?" Elk Tooth asked through Burning Ridge's English. "This cannot be. There is a white-man's paper. It says no man can build here, no man turn the soil, only come, look, take the yellow metal, and the Shoshone come to hunt. This is how it has been. This we have kept faith with."

"That ain't the way it is from now on," John Duffey's harsh voice brayed. "You redskins are gonna have to move out. We're taking what we want, when and where we want. This is no longer your land."

Confused, the older members of the deputation chattered among themselves. "Has the treaty been taken away? Why weren't we told?" they asked anxiously.

"No business of yours," Bull Grayson rumbled. "Weren't never your land to begin with. All this, the whole kaboodle, belongs to us white folk. By, ah, by, ah, right of conquest."

"We did not fight a war," the Shoshone said flatly.

"Naw, but we did . . . with the Mezkins. They lost, we won. So you an' all this land belongs to us now. Pack on out of here, before you get in trouble," Bull Grayson ordered.

Recognizing the futility of further dispute, Elk Tooth signaled his companions to turn around and leave. The council would want to hear this. They wouldn't like it, but they would have to hear. With all the dignity they could gather around them, the Shoshone slowly walked their horses toward the edge of the clearing. They had almost reached the shelter of the treeline when John Duffey snorted with irritation.

"Awh, hell. Them damned red niggers are takin' too much on themselves. It's time they learned who's boss."

He and two of his hand-picked henchmen ran to their horses and set out after the retreating Shoshone. Nearing the delegation, they drew their sidearms and rode in among the Indians, firing at point-blank range. Horses reared and squealed in fright, dust rose to mingle

31

with the powder smoke. Bullets slapped into flesh, and blood sprayed in the air. Two Shoshone fell dead. Duffey clubbed another in the side of the head with his sixgun and fired a blast into Fox Killer's face, blowing off the back of his head. Then the fighting ended in a flash.

Although wounded, the surviving Shoshone braves heeled their ponies into a gallop and disappeared over the ridge of the mountain. Cursing them, John Duffey watched for a while, then turned back to camp.

No denying it, Denver had lost its glitter. Changed by her out-of-body experience, and still aching because of her estrangement from Gaylen Stanton, Rebecca Caldwell walked Blake Street alone. She had no idea where she must go to encounter Chris Starret. Her final question to Bent Horn had elicited only that it was not in the Three Corners area of the Green River. As she passed the City House Hotel, she chanced to see a familiar broad back; Gaylen Stanton, once again in the blue uniform of the city police. She changed direction quickly and found herself in a notions shop.

A relatively new convenience on the sprawling frontier, the small shops sold newspapers, dime novels, women's cosmetics, tobacco products, neck scarves, tortoiseshell combs, and other items of convenience. Agitated by her near-encounter with Gaylen, Rebecca tried to cover her ruffled nature by feigning a casual examination of the array of newspapers. Most appeared rather prosaic, the more so for being from some of the wildest frontier communities. One headline drew her notice enough that she bent and lifted a copy from the display:

INDIANS ATTACK LOGGING CAMP

The paper, she noticed, was the Phoenix *Sun*. Her first impression was that such an event could hardly be considered unusual. The Apaches, Piutes, and some northern Navaho still made war on the whites. Any of them could be responsible. Quickly she scanned the opening paragraphs. Shoshone. The tribe's name might as well have been in boldface. Tucking the folded gazette under one arm, she walked to the counter and put down a nickle.

"That'll be eight cents here, ma'am," the young, bored clerk informed her.

"It clearly says five cents on the front page," Rebecca protested.

"This is Denver, ma'am, not Phoenix," the attendant said rudely, pointing to a sign over the newspaper display. "OUT OF TOWN JOURNALS, $.08," it read.

Rebecca placed another three pennies on the counter and left the shop. Frowning slightly, she concentrated on what she had learned. Shoshone warriors attacked a logging camp north of Flagstaff . . . where was Flagstaff? The name meant nothing to her. People set up towns nearly anywhere lately. Pushing, always pushing. What importance could it have? Chris Starret had been involved with stirring up the Shoshone in western Wyoming. Did that have any bearing? Bent Horn said the northern Shoshone were not involved, which might rule out Starret. At least she had a way of verifying that. She would see to that first, then look a little further.

Chapter 4

Women and girls still wailed in mournful tremolo, giving vent to their grief over the deaths of brave men. Boy-children went around with long faces and didn't laugh, shout, or whistle. In the big lodge of Walks Around, the council of the southern Shoshone met in solemn consideration of the demands for war. Walks Around and his son stood for peace. Many low, angry grumbles answered them. Desperate to make his point, Walks Around spoke again.

"Our people have been at peace with the whites since I was a little boy. Many of you know that. Some of you on this council provided eyes for the bluecoats in the time when the whites made war on the Mexicans, and again when they fought each other. Some of our young men are doing so now. How can we turn our backs on them and show bad faith to the whites by going to war?"

"What of the murder of our men? We took no fight to the whites. They killed our brothers with treachery. Our hunting grounds are bleeding and dying with the sap that runs from fallen trees. Are we still men if we allow this?" Many Horses demanded.

"My father speaks true," Red Shirt declared, trying to force more authority into his voice than he felt. "I know I lack the age and wisdom of many here, but even I see what all should consider. There are many whites living around us now. Only a few have done wrong. If we must fight, it should be only against those who deserve punishment."

Other voices rose, each according to his relative age.

35

While they parlayed, Walks Around's grandson, White Rabbit, addressed three of his small friends. His button nose wrinkled as he spoke with enthusiasm.

"The council makes big talk, angry words. While they do, we must be quiet and have no fun."

"It is the rule," Cross-Eyes reminded him.

White Rabbit made a face. "My father is on the council and my grandfather is chief of the council. I can do as I wish. And I wish . . . I wish to see the white-eyes. I want to see the trees falling and the land dying. How does land die? Who will go with me?"

"I," Sweet Grass shouted, copper face alight with eagerness.

"And I." Stone Boy hurried to align himself with White Rabbit.

Eyes aglow with the honor he gained by this, the ten-year-old put an arm on each of his friends. "What about you, Cross-Eyes?"

Cross-Eyes scuffed the toe of one moccasin against the hard ground. "I—I—ah . . . yes. I want to know why the pale ones are cutting down so many trees."

Afire with the spirit of adventure, White Rabbit jumped up and down. "Then hurry. Go and fetch your ponies. We will ride off to see the white-eyes."

"They ain't even Shoshone," a stubble-bearded man with a cast in one eye remarked.

"What difference does it make?" John Duffey growled in a low tone.

Crouched in the tall grass at the top of a low hill, the two men looked down on a glade filled with blackberry bushes. Two Ute women moved gracefully among the fruit-bearing vines, artfully avoiding the long, painful thorns. Each carried a woven willow basket into which she dumped the fruit as she picked it. Their palms had become purpled with berry juice.

"So we're gonna ride down there and say howdy, is that it?"

Duffey gave the wall-eyed man a contemptuous sneer. "Might be you'd rather prod cows for a living, Johnson?"

"Ah, now, Blackjack . . ." Marv Johnson began to protest.

"Chris told us to stir up the Indians. Here's a chance to stir up some more, once we kill off those squaws."

Marv Johnson's left hand squeezed his crotch. "Somethin' I'd like doin' more than killin' 'em."

Duffey considered it a moment. "You'll have your chance. Let's get back to the others."

Five minutes later, seven mounted men from Chris Starret's gang trotted out of the trees and surrounded the berry glade. Three dismounted and gave laughing chase to the startled, thoroughly frightened Ute women. They made a game of it, teasing as they moved in. Slowly they narrowed the distance until one long-armed hardcase could reach out and snag the fringed sleeve of a Ute beaded doeskin dress. The young woman inside the garment screamed with the force of a tormented soul in Hell.

"Whooiee," her assailant exclaimed. "This one's shore got spunk."

"Flop her down, Herbie, and give her some of yourn," a companion suggested with a leer.

"Don't talk dirty, Jude, they's ladies present," Herbert Graham chided with a snicker.

"I ain't talkin' dirty, it's you brought up spunk."

"Get the job done, God damn it," John Duffey snarled impatiently.

"Sure, Blackjack, sure," Jude responded. At his signal, playtime ended and the trio closed in on the frightened women.

"What do you want with us?" the other Ute woman demanded in her own tongue.

"None o' that turkey-gabble, sister," Herbie said with a chuckle as he reached for the neckline of her dress.

Doeskin ripped at the seams, and the young Ute shrieked in terror with the realization of what these white men had in mind. She flailed with small, ineffectual fists and kicked Herbie's shins. He lifted her with big, hard hands and had her on her back and on the ground before his companions caught her friend. A knee pinning each of her thighs widely apart, Herbie opened his fly and exposed a short, fat, blunt-tipped penis, reddened and rigidly erect. His victim whimpered and then screamed as he lowered himself in a rush and penetrated her.

Hot and tearing, his evil instrument violated her last secrets, ripping tissues and scouring the walls of her vagina. She writhed and screamed, the sound turning to howls as Herbie pumped and gyrated atop her. Jude had the other one down. Her feet and legs trembled in the air as he savagely thrust his long, slim organ back and forth. It didn't take long. When the pair of rapists cried out their completion and spasmed to shuddering halts, two more eager outlaws took their places.

"When you get done there, cut their throats and leave them," John Duffey commanded.

Rebecca Caldwell climbed the gray granite steps of the Central Post Office in downtown Denver. Inside she went to the Western Union office. She selected a pad of message forms and a pencil and wrote out a message in neat block letters.

Her telegram was addressed to Lieutenant Arthur Trapp at the Standing Rock outpost, Wyoming Territory. She made the message terse and explicit.

"Rumor suggests Chris Starret escaped death in mine. Please provide information. Are there any indications of unrest among Arapaho or Shoshone in Three Corners area? Wire reply. Rebecca Caldwell, Brown Palace Hotel, Denver."

Reading over her effort, Rebecca smiled with grim satisfaction and stepped to the counter. Within a few days she would know.

Nearly as fast as the white man's talking wire, word of

the impending war in the south reached Chief Shining Horse of the northern Shoshone. The three messengers from Chief Walks Around were given food and a place to rest while Shining Horse pondered the difficulties this presented. There could not be war; that much he believed ardently. The recent trouble with the Arapaho and the renegade whites led by the man Starret had proved that. His people had accepted the whites into their land, here and in the south. They could not turn back on their word. To the aging civil chief that meant as much, perhaps even more, than how badly the whites outnumbered them. Nor could he ignore his brother chief's request for help. Somehow he had to achieve that without adding to the chances of an uprising.

Caught up in the conundrum, he stayed up far into the night considering the alternatives. Revelation came to him like a lightning bolt. Had they not come to the brink of intertribal war only a short while ago? And had not peace been brought through the efforts of a certain person? *Sinaskawin*, the warrior woman of the Oglala, had blunted the arrows and checked the lances of Arapaho and Shoshone alike along the Green River. She had made an end of the man Starret, also. Although, Shining Horse reflected, he had heard that the renegade Starret had survived his supposed death and had gone somewhere in the southland. Could it be that he worked his evil in the land of the Utes and Southern Shoshone? *Sinaskawin* could find out.

Rousing his best message bearers early the next morning, he saw that they had swift ponies and ample supplies. Two of the three could speak the white man's English. That was good, Shining Horse thought as he prepared them for their task.

"Ride to the place of Standing Rocks. At the bluecoat outpost there, see the Smiling Soldier-Chief, Arthurtrapp. Learn from him where to find the White Robe Woman of the Red Top Oglala."

*   *   *

"See the trees!" White Rabbit squeaked in an excited whisper. "See them falling down."

Crouched in the tall grass halfway down the mountain side behind the logging camp, where they had wormed their way on hands and knees, the four Shoshone boys had their first close look at the strange white men who cut trees. Cross-Eyes lay next to White Rabbit and turned a scornful expression on the self-appointed leader of their adventure.

"What makes you think it's so exciting?" he asked with a sneer.

"'Exciting?'" White Rabbit retorted haughtily. "Playing with rattlesnakes is exciting. This is *dangerous.*"

"Yes, all those white-eyes around so close," Sweet Grass defended his friend. "They have guns and metal axes, better than our flint ones. They make it dangerous."

"It's going to be more dangerous, too," White Rabbit assured his detractor, inventing as he spoke. "We're— we're going right down there among them. Or are you afraid, Cross-Eyes?"

Cross-Eyes glowered at the others. "I am not afraid of anything. If you're so smart, why don't you lead us down there?" he taunted.

Laughing inside himself, White Rabbit answered with a grin. "We will go and count coup on the white men. And steal horses."

"Yes, and some of their food. I can smell it from here, and it makes my belly ache with hunger," Stone Boy added.

White Rabbit and Sweet Grass groaned. "You always think of your belly, Stone Boy," White Rabbit complained. "Why didn't you leave your appetite at home?"

"What?" the chubby Shoshone youth whispered in mock surprise, as he rubbed his bare belly. "And miss something good to eat?"

Wriggling through the grass, the boys glided in among the fallen trees. There they could come to their knees and advance at a faster pace. White Rabbit's heart pounded in his chest and he grinned reflexively, revealing to a knowing eye a good measure of fear mixed with his excitement. For three years he and his friends, like the other boys in camp, had practiced the stalking skills of their grown-up models, the hunters and warriors. Now they employed them in a game far more serious than those they had played among the lodges and familiar woods of home. Their course brought them close enough that the cooking odors tormented all of them.

Sweet Grass had forethought enough to have brought along enough ash cakes and jerky for a single day. It had taken that and more to reach their goal. Now four bellies rumbled in reaction to the prospect of food so tantalizingly near. In the lead, White Rabbit halted abruptly. His companions jolted to a stop in chain reaction. With one hand he motioned them to join him.

"We will steal food and eat, then we take horses and ride for home," White Rabbit excitedly told his friends.

"If we make coup on some of the white-eyes, maybe the war chief will make us warriors," Sweet Grass gulped, eyes bright.

"We're too little," Cross-Eyes dashed his hopes. Then he grinned at a perceived certainty. "But the singers will tell of our deeds for all time."

"Then we'll do it," White Rabbit declared, though it sounded more like a question.

Lupe Bargas had been a cook for all his adult life. Before that he had been apprenticed to his *Tio Ramón* since his tenth year. Lupe had taken the job with the gringos because it paid good money. He never knew men who could eat so much. Every morning the loggers wanted beefsteak, potatoes, eggs, and the sweet, thick tortillas they called flapjacks. In Mexico a man could live a week on what each of them consumed at a single meal. At midday they wanted more beefsteak, bigger than the first, with potatoes, white beans and ham, dry corn soaked in milk and stewed to make it soft again, and

41

loaves of fresh bread. Evening was no different, except that then they wanted pies and sweet puddings to go with all the rest.

Well, Lupe reflected, he had two assistant cooks to help him. Even if they were gringos and naturally lazy, he got enough work out of them to put the meals on the table. At least it allowed him to take his siesta, like any reasonable man would, while they and the two swampers cleaned up and started preparing the next mountain of food. Only sometimes they were careless and stupid.

He had told them to set two gang-loaf pans of bread out to cool on the screened back porch of the cook shack. Lupe saw only one. Where was the other? Muttering to himself, he set off to find the assistants. He found one of them peeling onions, a job a swamper should be doing. The other, he was told, had gone to the outhouse—the *escusado.*

"*¡Mierda!* If I could get the work of one out of the two of you I would be satisfied," Lupe complained. "Leave that to the boy to do. We have roasts to slice." Grumbling, Lupe led the way into the kitchen.

"*¿Que est esto?* What is this?" He stared in wonderment at the warming shelf of the big wood range. "I cooked four big roasts of beef. I took four out of the oven. Now there are but three."

"Them loggers is hungry bastards," one cook mumbled sullenly.

"True. But they do not steal. What does this mean?"

Seated on the bare ground among the skirted pilings that kept the mess hall level on the mountain slope, White Rabbit and his friends licked greasy fingers and wiped them on their bare bellies. The meat had tasted good, hot and sweet and juicy. It went well with the strange brown lumps with the white, fluffy insides. It made Sweet Grass think of the fry bread his mother made—something she had learned from the white-eye woman at the agency. Satisfied, their stomachs stretched

42

to the point of discomfort, the boys looked at each other with the highlights of adventure dancing in their black eyes.

"Now we go for the horses," White Rabbit decided.

"Why not sleep first, like our fathers and brothers do after a feast?" Stone Boy suggested.

"Do you want to be caught?" Cross-Eyes scolded. "We are in the enemy camp. You snore so loud they would find us in a flash. White Rabbit is right. We steal horses, take the rabbit-ears, too."

White Rabbit thought of the many rabbit-ear ponies—mules—used to drag logs away after the white-eyes trimmed the branches. They didn't ride well, but they tasted good. Yes, they'd take them, too.

"We'll go now," he commanded.

Like gophers popping from a burrow, the Shoshone boys exited by way of a loose piece of skirting. Bent low, they started across the open space toward the hastily constructed corral that contained most of the livestock. They had gained some thirty yards when White Rabbit heard the hard pounding of booted feet behind them. A huge hand swooped past his side and grabbed him about the waist. Suddenly he found himself running on air.

"Look what I've got!" a booming voice shouted.

"Hold him. Get them all. Don't let them get away," Lupe Bargas called from the kitchen porch. "They stole the meat—I know it."

Struggling against the tight, painful clutch of the logger, White Rabbit managed to give his captor a hard rap in one eye with his elbow. The hold loosened, and the small Shoshone sprang free.

"Run!" he shouted unnecessarily to his friends. White Rabbit ran another ten feet before a powerful blow set him staggering to fall face first as hot agony spread through his side. Only faintly he heard the report of the revolver that had shot him.

"There they go. Get 'em! Shoot 'em down!" another voice bellowed.

John Duffey eased his sights in line with Stone Boy

43

and squeezed the trigger. The big .45 slug struck the little lad in the small of his back, severing his spine. He flopped foward on the ground, twitching like a bug impaled on a pin. Sweet Grass screamed and began to weep, cursing himself for his weakness. He was terrified. Cross-Eyes bounded far ahead of all of them. He ducked and dodged and worked to keep the corral of horses and mules directly behind him to prevent any chance shots.

Near one end of the rail fence he vaulted the top bar and disappeared among the milling livestock. Angry shouts followed him. John Duffey walked leisurely over to the boy he had killed. He looked down in disgust and spat a stream of tobacco juice onto Stone Boy's back.

"Goddamn Injun brats," he snarled.

"*Oye, hombres,* I got one!" Lupe Bargas shouted triumphantly as he tottered back toward the mess hall.

Slung over one shoulder, kicking and wriggling, Sweet Grass yelled in Shoshone to be released. His vigorous movements put his slightly built Mexican captor off balance. Lupe used his free hand to swat the boy's rump. The sharp, stinging sensation in his buttocks halted Sweet Grass' struggles. He had never in his life experienced a spanking, but he knew the purpose with a single smack.

"One of them got away," the logging foreman announced as men gathered from all directions, to stand gawking in front of the mess hall.

"This one's shot up some, but he'll live," a faller declared, looking down at White Rabbit.

"Let's lock 'em in that little toolshed," the foreman suggested.

"Naw," John Duffey drawled. "Why not finish them off right now?"

The bleak looks of the working men made a distinct impression on Blackjack Duffey that he had gone a bit too far. No matter. He'd have his way sooner or later, and the red skin vermin would be disposed of.

Chapter 5

Dust swirled in brown clouds that rolled over the spotted rumps of the Shoshone ponies and obscured the riders momentarily. A steady southwest breeze blew it away, and the leader of the trio spoke to the uniformed sentry in fair English lacking in inflection.

"We come to see the Smiling Soldier Chief."

"Y'all mean Lieutenant Trapp?" the soldier from Tupelo, Mississippi, drawled his question as he scratched at the cotton-white hair that stuck straight out below his *kepi*.

"He is in charge?" the copper-skinned warrior asked.

"He is here at Standing Rock," the Southern lad admitted.

"We will speak with him."

"Well, that depends on whether he'll speak with you," the amused guard said with a snicker.

"I'll speak with them, Trooper. And why didn't you summon the corporal of the guard?"

Startled, the young soldier stiffened into a position of attention. "Sir, yes, sir. Sir, they just sorta popped up out of nowhere, sir."

"Does the phrase 'keeping always on the alert and observing everything within sight and hearing' mean anything to you?"

"Sir, yes, sir. It's part of my First General Order, sir."

45

"Then perhaps you need more experience in its practical application. Stand aside and let these men pass."

Still rattled, the green trooper complied with alacrity. Lieutenant Trapp produced his boyish smile. He addressed the warriors in the Athapascan dialect of the Shoshone.

"You come from Chief Shining Horse?"

Surprise flickered on the spokesman's face. "You knew of our coming?"

"No. But I recognized the clothing style and beadwork of the Shoshone. Men of such proud independence would not come without being sent. Come with me, we will talk."

Young Arthur Trapp, who had come West to win glory in an Indian war, had indeed done a lot of growing up. With the help of the strange young woman, *Sinaskawin*, he had opened his eyes to the nature and problems of the Indians. His sincere efforts to fairly administer their reservations, and his willing testimony that had sent his former executive officer to Leavenworth Federal Penitentiary, earned him the respect of the tribal leaders. Young Lieutenant Trapp took deserved pride in his accomplishments—in particular, the learning of his charges' language. Walking with his visitors as equals, he led them across the parade ground.

In his office, Lieutenant Trapp provided coffee with plenty of sugar, then listened to the reason for their visit. He nodded and gave them a big grin. After calling an orderly to replenish the coffee, he folded his hands on top of his desk and spoke slowly in his newly acquired language.

"Chief Shining Horse is fortunate. I have heard from White Robe Woman recently. She is in the white man's village called Denver. I know," he went on, raising a hand to stop protests. "Nothing to worry about. Even though your people and the Arapaho around Denver are not on the best of terms, and—I might add—you are off the reservation now and would be in even more danger to go there, she can still be reached and informed of what concerns Chief Shining Horse. The talking wire will send word to her. We should have an answer before the sun goes to sleep in the western hills."

Astonishment printed itself on the three warriors' faces. "This great medicine is possible? You control the forces of the wire?"

Lieutenant Trapp's open hand concealed his slight smile. "Not I. But there is a man here at Standing Rock who knows the ways of the talking wire. Come, you can watch while I have him send your message."

In the telegraph office, the Shoshone warriors looked on with awe while Lieutenant Trapp made the talking marks on paper. Then they gaped openly in wonder while the telegrapher clattered his key and received acknowledgment of receipt of the message.

"There," Lieutenant Trapp said breezily. "Now shall we find something to eat?"

Fire burned in Cross-Eyes' chest. He gasped for air and panted as he ran through the thick stand of birch. He had ridden his pony into the ground earlier in the day and left the exhausted animal to fend for itself. Sweat slicked his body and ran stingingly into his eyes. At least he recognized this landmark, and his heart swelled with relief. He had only a short way to go.

That was good. His dry mouth felt like he had eaten sand. His legs ached, and he had grown weak in the knees. Cross-Eyes remembered again the scene of horror he'd witnessed in the camp of the white men.

Stone Boy had been running only a few paces behind him. Angry shouts rose on all sides. Then Stone Boy had cried out and Cross-Eyes had looked back to see the boy's belly rip open in a welter of blood. Cross-Eyes' friend had fallen and twitched like a frog with a broken back. Screaming, Cross-Eyes had continued to run until he'd reached their ponies, hidden behind a low hill. He'd waited, frightened but not wanting to abandon his friends. When no one came, he knew what had to be done.

Swiftly he mounted and rode away at a gallop. When his pony played out, he kept going. Now the steep incline sucked at his last vestiges of strength. He was, after all, "only a little boy." His mother's favorite phrase dragged at him, offered reason to stop, to sit down and rest. Cross-Eyes fought it, and reached the top of the ridge. Hope gave new energy to his numb legs. There, spread out in the valley below, was the summer hunting village of his people.

Cross-Eyes staggered on, and finally reached the chest-deep stream at the foot of the slope. He kicked off his moccasins, shed his breechcloth, and threw himself into the cool water. With leaden arms he flailed at it, gulping some to cool the fires that raged inside. His vision blurred. Oh, no, he thought desperately. Not now. You can't cry like a baby. A few more strokes. His toes touched the pebbly bottom. With a weak shout of triumph, Cross-Eyes surged out of the water. He made a dozen steps before the scene around him began to whirl and a spot of blackness grew to engulf him.

He came to almost at once, or at least it seemed like that to him. Walks Around and several men bent anxiously over the small lad. "You have been with the Spirits for a hand-breadth of the day, boy. Tell us what you know," the chief commanded.

Quickly, fighting tears of grief and terror, Cross-Eyes related all that had happened. He told of White Rabbit's desire to go see the white men who cut trees, and how they gathered food for the journey and slipped out to their ponies. Then he described the cutting place and the terrible things that happened. Red Shirt, father of White Rabbit, grunted in smoldering anger and muttered a black medicine curse on the whites. When Cross-Eyes completed his narrative, he could clearly read the grief and rage in Walks Around's eyes.

"You do not know if my grandson lives?" he pressed the boy.

"No. He was shot first. Then Stone Boy was killed. I waited for them to slip away and come to the ponies. No one came." Cross-Eyes hung his head in shame and sorrow.

"It is not your fault, boy," Walks Around consoled him. Of the elders and young men, he asked, "What now?"

"We go and kill the whites," Red Shirt shouted. "Drive them all from our lands."

Still disinclined to make war on the whites indiscriminately, Walks Around looked sadly at his son. He understood Red Shirt, for his own loss weighed heavily in his chest. White Rabbit shot and possibly dead . . . his favorite grandchild, though he would never admit it openly.

"We cannot kill just any whites," Walks Around counseled. "That way leads only to trouble."

"He is your grandson," Red Shirt snarled in growing fury. "Have you no desire for revenge?"

Walks Around nodded solemnly. "I do. But the taking of lives among those not responsible will bring us more grief than vengeance."

"Then what can we do?" Red Shirt asked scornfully.

"I will draft an explanation to the White Father and to the Bluecoat Chief. One of the young men who know the white man's marks on paper can do that for me. In it I will say who broke the treaty with our people and what we do about it. Then I will take up the war pipe and lead the men against the ones who murdered one child of our tribe and made captive of two others. The bad whites will have their blood flow freely. This I promise you. I have spoken."

Rebecca Caldwell answered a rap on her hotel room

49

door to reveal a gangling youth in his mid-teens with buck teeth and ratty, moss-hued hair. "Telegram for ya, ma'am," he announced.

Surprised to find a messenger boy of such advanced age, Rebecca accepted the yellow envelope and handed the lad a dime tip. He grinned lopsidedly and boldly eyed her alluring curves and breastline. It encouraged her to exercise her temper.

"Aren't you a little old for your job?" she inquired.

"Yep. I'm studyin' to be an operator. Learnin' Mr. Morse's code. This time next year I'll be a telegraph agent."

That response prodded Rebecca's conscience. "Well, I wish you good luck at it, then," she offered lamely.

Alone again, she tore open the envelope. Lieutenant Arthur Trapp's message served to confirm what her experience with Bent Horn had illuminated. It also prompted her to seek more information regarding the Indian conflict around Flagstaff in Arizona Territory. Asking around, she soon learned of two new arrivals in Denver who had come from Flagstaff. She located them at their hotel, the Windsor, in the Gentlemen's Bar.

"Yes, Miss Caldwell, we have just come from Flagstaff, on our way to Chicago," a portly gentleman in the fashionable suit of a businessman informed her.

"I understand there is some Indian trouble there?" she pressed.

"Well, ah, yes. There has been a skirmish or two, but that's been confined to some savages out hunting, as I understand, and some of Big Mac Kellogg's loggers."

"Who is this Kellogg?"

"New man in the community, though I suppose you could say we all are. He's set up a sawmill and is cutting trees to provide lumber for the rather healthy spurt of construction in the northern part of the territory."

The man was either a land speculator or a town boomer, Rebecca decided. "You say he's in the lumber business? My impression of Arizona is of desert. Are there enough trees to make a lasting business?"

Chuckling indulgently, the rotund gentlemen exchanged glances. "My dear young woman, there is hardly anything else around Flagstaff beside trees," the stout one's friend advised her. "Oh, there's some mining, but nothing like the Comstock in Virginia City, or the California gold fields of thirty years ago. As the market for copper grows, we'll no doubt see some boom in that direction, plenty of it. I think with that in mind, more than anything else, the Santa Fe Railroad put through a main line to connect Chicago with the Southern Pacific spur to San Bernardino, California, and thus to Los Angeles."

"You're probably right, Myron. Because why anyone would want to go into Los Angeles is beyond me. Not even a decent seaport close at hand. Of course, with the railroad, land values around Flagstaff have already begun to increase. Before long they'll soar. Anyone who wants to invest, now's the time."

Rebecca congratulated herself on her astute judgment. Perhaps their loquacity would help her in learning more. "You described these Indian battles as small skirmishes with Kellogg's men. Where did this happen? And do you know what Indians were involved?"

"Nothing to worry about if you're planning to go to Flagstaff. It happened a good two-days' journey north of town through rugged mountains. Outside of a few blanket Indians, Pimas and a few Utes, you never seen Indians in Flagstaff. Shoshone never come that far south. It was Shoshone who attacked Kellogg's loggers."

"You've been most kind," Rebecca informed them, turning on her charm. "And you've relieved my concern about Indians. One other thing. Are you familiar with a man by the name of Starret? Chris Starret?"

"Umm, no. Not that I recall. At least, not in Flagstaff," Myron told her.

"Nor I. It'd be a name a man would remember. Starret . . . no, certainly not one of the founders of the

51

town, like Myron and myself. Is he in business?"

"Not like you gentlemen, certainly," Rebecca responded. "He's a murderer and a thief."

"I—I—ah, say," Myron stammered.

Rebecca asked a few more questions about the town, thanked them, and departed. Several interesting facts began to spin webs in her thoughts. Indeed, land values would soar. And apparently this Kellogg had started the logging business on a large scale. The message from Chief Shining Horse said the Southern Shoshone were having trouble with men cutting trees. From the two Flagstaff boosters and her own knowledge, Rebecca knew well the value of lumber. If there was money to be made, in land or in lumber, Chris Starret could be counted on being in the middle of it. By the time she had traversed a block, Rebecca had made up her mind. She changed direction and headed for the main post office.

"What'll it be, ma'am?" the telegrapher inquired.

"I have a short message to be sent. It's to Chief Shining Horse, Shoshone Nation, care of Lieutenant Arthur Trapp, Standing Rock Outpost, Wyoming Territory. Say simply that I am headed for Flagstaff, Arizona Territory, and to pass the word to the Southern Shoshone. Sign it—and I'll tell you how to spell it—*Sinaskawin.*"

Chris Starret took John Duffey and Bull Grayson aside in the rose-cast light of sunset. He had returned to the logging operation to learn of the captive children. At first he saw it as an advantage. On longer reflection, he saw a possibly fatal flaw in holding the Indian boys.

"You hadn't much choice at the time, I understand that," he told the nominal leaders of the hardcases working for Kellogg. "The thing is, we're likely to get a lot of attention from the Shoshone. If the Shoshone concentrate their attacks on us, their agent might well start listening to their complaints. The army, too. In which case we're in trouble. What you have to do is spread the trouble around a little. Get the redskins mad enough to go after any whites, wherever they find them."

"You have any ideas?" John Duffey queried.

"Nothing solid," Chris admitted. "I'm sure you two can come up with something. Chances are you have some time to plan what you want to do. Now, another little matter has come up. Big Mac is cutting more trees. A hell of a lot of them are government property."

"He's got to," Bull Grayson defended his employer. "To meet all those orders you took."

"Damn. He doesn't need to do that. We can scam those people and pull out of here with a huge profit."

"Like I said before, Big Mac don't like doing business that way," Grayson reminded him. "Besides, slash cutting drives those savages wild. They say the ground will wash away, all the game leave."

"They're right," Chris admitted. "But, who cares? By then we'll be long gone. If it aggravates the Indians, it accomplishes our purpose anyway. But there's a lot of open land to be harvested, if Kellogg insists on filling those contracts."

After dismissing Kellogg's chief henchmen, Chris gave thought to his railroad spur confidence game. Before leaving Phoenix, he had over a hundred thousand dollars pledged and deposits of thirty thousand. It made him feel so sure he had a foolproof scheme that he wanted to gather in even more before departing. Big Mac Kellogg's operation could run without him and John Duffey. They could be taking in the high style of San Francisco while someone else did the dirty work, all the while watching the profits grow. When the fraud was eventually discovered, if Kellogg got caught in the middle, too bad for him.

Chapter 6

"A feller'd think all this cuttin' would drive the birds away," Linsey Fellows observed to his topping partner.

"Yep, Lin, but lissen to 'em. Just a-warblin' away."

From all sides of the logging area and camp north of Flagstaff, birdcalls filled the air. While the two loggers chattered as they walked to the next tree to be topped out, the melodious sound increased in quantity. Abruptly it ceased, coming as it did from the throats of Shoshone warriors, to be replaced by fierce war cries.

"Holy Christ," Linsey shouted. "It's Injuns! We're bein' attacked!" He started to shout a warning only to have the alarm cut off before it could begin: an arrow transfixed his throat.

Beside him, his companion received two arrows in the chest, one of which pierced his heart. At once the underbrush swarmed with bronze bodies as one contingent of painted warriors rushed forward on foot, backed up by mounted braves with rifles. Here and there torches flickered among the attackers. Under covering fire, they advanced toward the buildings. Here and there shots and screams sounded as the disorganized loggers began to rally and give resistance.

One burly faller reared up and gave his broad-headed ax a full roundhouse swing. Its keen edge made a meaty smack as it bit into a Shoshone neck, severing it. The head went bounding. Completing his follow-through, the logger went after another enemy, hickory handle held at high port, blade dripping blood.

He bowled over a slightly built Shoshone and made a disdainful one-hand swing to split the Indian's ribs and his heart. Hot pain erupted in the logger's right leg as an arrow buried deep into the thigh muscle. He turned in that direction, his face puckered against the discomfort. Before he could locate his assailant, a trade rifle blasted from ten feet away and the big .56-caliber ball pulped his brain.

With whoops and hollers, the mounted warriors drummed their ponies to a gallop and swept through the disrupted camp. Two more loggers died screaming, lance points driven through their bodies. Bull Grayson began to organize his gunhands, and soon controlled fire answered the wild charge of the Shoshone.

"Goddamn, there's sure a lot of 'em," one gunhawk observed.

"More than we've got time to deal with," Bull admitted. "Look, them two set the tool shed afire."

His subordinate blanched. "Oh, Lordy, help us. I—I left near a case of dynamite in there."

"If it isn't capped, it won't do a dang thing," Grayson growled. "You know that."

"It'll burn like the fires of Hell. An' I ain't so sure I didn't leave a box of caps along with."

Already the majority of the loggers, not seasoned fighting men, had begun to retreat toward the sawmill farther down the mountain. There they would find, they correctly figured, safety in numbers. Among them ran several of John Duffey's picked men. His mind on the large amount of dynamite, Bull Grayson led the way with his enforcers.

They walked half-turned, firing behind them, at a steady pace. When the fuse caps ignited, sympathetic detonation set off the dynamite. The blast lifted the burning roof from the shack, while the blazing walls disintegrated in a great shower of flame-bright splinters.

Shocked and confused by the unexpected explosion, the Shoshone warriors cried out in consternation and broke off the attack. They streamed into the woods to regroup. Several of the men and their ponies who had been close to the center of the tumult bore minor wounds from the flying shards of wood.

"They're gone!" one relieved logger shouted. "They turned tail and ran."

"That blast shook 'em right enough," another added.

"They'll be back," John Duffey stated grimly. "We pull back to the sawmill. Lots of lumber piles around there to use for defenses."

When the working men regrouped at the sawmill, Chris Starret came from the office to take charge. The fallers, log skinners, top-men, and drag-line men had been badly frightened. They had also developed a good hot edge of anger. More than a few had seen friends fall to the deadly fire of the Indians. They vowed to make the savages pay. Chris quickly took advantage of that mood.

"This is the second time Indians have attacked these camps. Are we going to let them get away with it?" he shouted loudly.

"Hell, no!" the workmen bellowed, led by the professional gunmen among them.

"They'll be back, you can be sure of that. We have to be ready for them. Drag those wagons in among the lumber stacks. Put one there, and over there, two in that big gap, another there . . ." Chris directed, describing an irregular figure on the ground that allowed overlapping fire from one jutting point to another, with deep, enfiladed cul-de-sacs between.

Yelling to one another, the workmen and gunhands set to with a will. John Duffey got one group busy filling tow sacks with dirt and rocks and adding them to the tops of the lumber piles to form firing parapets. The slightly wounded had their injuries treated and began to gather and redistribute ammunition among the defenders. Chris Starret seemed to be everywhere at once.

His advice received eager attention and immediate implementation. An hour passed with no sign of the Shoshone braves. Chris got teamsters to setting their draglines on uncut logs and dragging them into the open area around the defenses in an irregular pattern that would force men and horses to slow and take oblique approaches to the improvised battlements, thus exposing both to heavy fire for a longer time. A pall of dust rose over the mill site, giving an amber cast to the sunlight. The dragline men had nearly completed their field of obstructions when the Shoshone attacked again.

Many Horses and Red Shirt led the two wings of the Shoshone attack. At the center, Walks Around commanded the overall battle and directed the men on foot. He sat a fine Palouse, in full war regalia, a long, bead-decorated lance, with many dangling feathers along the shaft, held firmly across the animal's withers. With it he signaled the rudimentary tactics of the fight.

"There is someone among them who thinks like a soldier," Walks Around confided to the slender boy of fourteen who served as his messenger in the event they lost visual contact with any element.

"How is that?"

"See how he makes a fort of that wood? A white-eye, a wise Soldier Chief, once told me that to fight like that, without being able to move, is to pick one's place to die. But the white-eyes build them anyway. Today the Shoshone will teach that lesson to these whites."

"I want my knife to taste their blood," the young lad said eagerly.

Walks Around gave the boy a kindly smile. "There is time enough for that later on. Keep out of the way of the white-eyes' bullets so that you can carry my words to Red

58

Shirt and Many Horses."

"Oh, War Chief, why do you say that?"

Walks Around nodded in the direction of their distant camp. "Your father and mother would not like it if I brought you home lying across your pony's back. I would dislike it, too. Far too few boys are being born to our people anymore. You must grow and be strong if the Shoshone are to survive. Go and tell Red Shirt that we will attack before the white-eyes finish outside their strong place."

Through slitted eyes, Red Shirt looked at the camp. That first charge was for the honor of our people, he told himself. This is for my little boy. It might be that he could find where the white-eyes had hidden his son. And Sweet Grass, also, he reminded himself. If they are not dead already. The cold thought twisted in his gut like a knife. If they lived, if he managed to find the boys and free them, then all would be well. Honor would be avenged and they could go back to their summer hunting camp. *If.* Pondering the unknown gave him a thudding pain in his head. Red Shirt gritted his teeth and watched through a screen of branches for the signal from his father.

Walks Around raised his lance and turned it forward and back. Red Shirt's quirt lashed his pony's flank. With fearsome yells, he and his followers raced out of the trees. From carefully selected points along the edge of the standing forest, marksmen opened up with rifle fire that kept the defenders ducking. The mounted warriors reached the lumber stacks and produced yet another unexpected tactic.

Instead of riding about, firing as individuals, a dozen bowmen sat their ponies quietly, firing arching shafts into the defenses. Once their flight paths were assured, one in three of the projectiles had gobs of pine pitch and cattail tufts set alight and launched into the raw wood of the defenses. The bowmen laughed scornfully and called out insults in their own language as the white men cried in alarm and scurried about in attempts to extinguish the blazes. Thick black smoke began to obscure the scene.

Under its cover, Red Shirt and three trusted braves began a search of outbuildings. They uncovered one which showed signs of the boys being held there, but no other indication of where they might be. Angered, and grieving for his small son, Red Shirt abandoned the search when the whites began to gain advantage over the flames. With the other warriors, he obeyed Walks Around's signal to withdraw.

Toward late afternoon, a party of some fifteen men galloped into the beseiged lumber camp, led by Big Mac Kellogg. He went at once to where Chris Starret oversaw the defenses. He quickly learned that the Shoshone had come with every intention of staying until the job had been done. They had made three attacks so far and burned a considerable amount of freshly sawed lumber. Ammunition was running low.

"We have the manpower now," Chris urged Kellogg. "I say we wade in there now and kill them all. Then backtrail 'em and wipe out their village."

"No," Big Mac growled. "We wouldn't gain a thing by doing that. Might even lose some sympathy. It's good the way it is."

"How can you say that?" Chris barked back.

"We're the victims. We've got a perfect reason to appeal to the army to come to our aid. Start a big campaign, talk to the newspapers in town meetings, and get people stirred up. With all that on our side, we got everything right where we should."

"They'll burn this place down around our ears if we don't kill them or force them to run," Chris protested.

"What if they do? The troops will have to drive them out then. The army's contracted for lumber also."

While the argument progressed, Walks Around

signaled another attack. Whooping and firing into the defenses, the Shoshone charged the smoldering lumber stacks. Three more fires started. At last, Big Mac Kellogg wore down Chris Starret's insistence to exterminate the Indians.

"All right. I'll organize a counterattack, go after them before they have a chance to regroup. That should drive them off. Especially if we kill one or more of the leaders," said Chris.

He got his chance within ten minutes. Shouting hasty orders, he sent John Duffey and the gunmen to their mounts. Half a dozen armed loggers went along. Chris called for his horse and rode to face the semicircle of fighting men. He gave them a long, silent glance, weighing them for what they must do.

"Spread out and go after those devils at the gallop. We'll hit the center. That old man with the lance is leading them. A hundred dollars to the man who kills him."

"Then let's ride," one hardcase blurted.

Turning about, Chris set spurs in his mount's flanks and they leaped forward. As they progressed across the open ground, he kept shouting to his followers.

"Keep apart! Don't fire until we're right on them. Don't get ahead of the men on your sides."

At fifty yards they opened fire. Two bullets shattered the shaft of Walks Around's lance. Confronted with the unexpected, the Shoshone warriors raced away to consider this new tactic. The white gunmen gave chase. More hot lead cracked through the air. Two warriors fell from their war saddles. Many Horses placed himself between Walks Around and the whites risking his life for the elderly chief. A slug through the shoulder rewarded him.

Shaken, Many Horses steadied himself and urged greater speed. Dust rose from two dozen diverse trails. Chris shouted to his men to keep together. If they divided themselves too thin, they would be at the mercy of the

Indians. Cursing men threw poorly aimed rounds at the retreating Shoshone. Within eight minutes the Indians had been driven from the logging site. Victorious, though unsatisfied, Chris Starret led the men back to camp.

Rattling along the tracks, the rhythmic clack-clack of the rail joints as the coach trucks rolled over them lulled Rebecca Caldwell into a light dozing state. Aboard the Denver and Rio Grande every-other-day-run to Santa Fe, she had little to do but think about Chris Starret and what she might be hurrying toward. Such thoughts disturbed her enough that she made a directed effort to rouse from her drifting somnolence.

In the tiny cubicle of the convenience she dashed away the last threads of whispy lethargy with a few dabs of cool water. She had a task to occupy her time, she chided herself, one she had been putting off for too long. With the help of the porter, she set up the narrow table between the facing seats in her car. Obtaining a pen, paper, and inkwell from a pigeonhole arrangement at the front of the coach, she settled in to catch up on her domestic obligations.

"My dear son, Joey," Rebecca began her missive to her stepson, Joey Ridgeway. "I hope that this letter finds you in good health and doing well in your studies." *I hope that you're still single and haven't gotten the Parsons girl pregnant,* is what she really wanted to say. "Has Mrs. Parsons found a suitable school for you in Houston or San Antonio?" *He's nearly fifteen, and terribly bright, and should be in a good private academy.* That's what his father would have wanted, she acknowledged. "I miss the good times we had together and want to visit you soon. I am confident that I shall soon catch up to Chris Starret and put an end to his evil ways. When that is accomplished, I'll come back to you. Maybe we could spend a summer with Iron Calf's people. Would you like that?"

At twelve and thirteen, Joey had been fascinated by the

life of a Sioux boy. He already rode like a natural and soon learned to use a bow and arrows with consummate skill. He also gloried in wearing only moccasins and breechcloth from April to October. Although blatantly caucasian, with snowy blond hair, Joey quickly tanned as coppery brown as any Sioux boy and grew his hair into braids. Rebecca had had more than her share of problems when she had taken him from his Oglala friends to southeast Texas, not the least of those from his infatuation with Winona Parsons. Her determination to settle with Roger Styles had dictated the move.

It had ended in double tragedy. Although Roger Styles died, he had nurtured a protégé every bit as malevolent as his mentor. Chris Starret and Jim Elkhorn proceeded to terrorize a large part of Texas and murder Bob Russle. Rebecca put aside the pen, a sudden, unanticipated ache tearing at her heart. Oh, Bob—dear, sweet, devoted Bob. Her obsession had cost his life and her future happiness, and dashed her hopes for Joey. Behind it all lurked Chris Starret and the specter of Roger Styles' evil genius.

An emnity she wasn't aware of generating glowed in Rebecca Caldwell's eyes. "I'll get you this time, you son-of-a-bitch," she vowed.

Chapter 7

Šila walked haltingly and stiff-legged, still disoriented by the constant rocking of the livestock car in which he had ridden. A throng of small, brown people streamed around the big Palouse stallion and his owner, Rebecca Caldwell, in the streets of Santa Fe, New Mexico. Naturally enough, the depots of the rival railroads were located across town from each other. Since she would be leaving the next morning, Rebecca decided to trust her mount to the holding pen at the AT&SF station.

That is, until she saw it. There were no stalls for horses, not even a sun shade. Although located in a high mountain basin, Santa Fe nevertheless existed in a desert. Hot and dry at this time of year, this substandard corral offered no inducement to Rebecca. Disgusted with the casual attitude regarding such a lack of accommodations—a large, adobe-walled, thatched-roof shelter was "under construction" and would be "finished sometime soon"—she led Šila back to Ortega's City Livery. Then she set out to find a room for the night.

Tiled walks, red-brown in color, made of the local clay soil, served in the place of the usual boardwalks. They could hardly be distinguished from the roadway, except for deep, narrow drainage ditches at each side and the ubiquitous hitching rails. One such sidewalk led Rebecca under arched overhangs that the local merchants used as extensions of their shops to display their wares. Parrots and songbirds squawked and trilled in cages at one establishment, while the savory aroma of baked goods wafted from an open doorway of the next. Tightly woven sarapes and ponchos of wool and cactus fiber stirred in the breeze, their fringed hems brushing the raven hair on the top of Rebecca's head. Compared to the Anglo towns to the north, Santa Fe had a lively, refreshing atmosphere that Rebecca rather enjoyed.

"Hey, Hawk!" a youthful voice hailed from the next street corner.

A lean, stringy, broad-shouldered young man turned his head to answer the shouted greeting and nearly ran down Rebecca in the process. At the last instant he checked, which caused him to lurch off the walkway and come up hard against a tie-rail.

"Ow! Damn. Uh—pardon, ma'am," he blurted, face growing pink in his discomfort.

"Think nothing of it. It's as much my fault as anyone's. I was . . . gawking."

Now that they had come to rest, Rebecca studied the young man who seemed all elbows, knees, and sixgun. His steady gray eyes looked levelly back into her own widely set, intensely sapphire orbs. He had a nice smile, straight nose, and square chin. Rebecca chided herself for the little thrill of interest that rippled through her. He wore a battered, once-gray Stetson which covered a luxuriant head of dusty-brown hair that contained streaks of sun-bleached blond. Rebecca and the boy began to speak at the same time.

"That's kind . . ." And she, "I've just arr—"

"Pardon, ma'am, go right ahead," he invited, blushing.

"I've only arrived this morning in Santa Fe. I'm afraid I was gawking, not watching where I was going. My name's Rebecca Caldwell."

"You're most forgiving, Miss Rebecca. That feller hollered at me and took my mind off where I was going.

That's the trouble in my business; everyone gets to know you. I'm Aaron Hawkins."

"How do you do—ah . . ." she paused. "That man called you Hawk, I believe?"

"Nickname," Aaron gave through a shy smile. "Comes with my calling, I'm afraid."

"Whereupon, since you mentioned it twice, I suppose I should ask what you do for a living," Rebecca responded, teasing. "I'd gather you are a politician."

Aaron looked wounded to the core. "Oh, no, ma'am—uh—Miss Rebecca. I'm in an honest trade."

He pulled aside his square-cut, dark brown coat to expose his vest and the circle badge with the star inside it. *United States Marshal* was deeply engraved in the rim and painted black, with *Deputy* across the star, the number "27" below it. Rebecca's eyes grew wide and round. Her full, sensuous lips pursed, then spread in a fulsome smile.

"How do you do, Marshal Hawkins?"

Belatedly, Aaron snatched the hat from his head with a big, thick-fingered hand and held it to his chest. "Oh, no need to be formal. I'm just—Aaron, or Hawk, if you prefer."

Rebecca did something with her smile that enhanced the loveliness of her heart-shaped face. "Aaron is a lovely name. Do you work out of Santa Fe?"

"Yes—yes, I do." For obvious reasons he felt compelled to keep the conversation going. "I'm making arrangements to leave on a trip to the west, though. Out to Flagstaff, in Arizona Territory. It's business."

"How extraordinary. I'm going there on tomorrow's train. Is your, ah, business connected to the Indian trouble I've heard about?"

"No. That's not my jurisdiction. There's been some murders I'm to look into. And some people have complained that they have been driven off their land. Say, our meeting is remarkable. I'm taking the same train. Why don't we talk about it over coffee? I was on my way for some, and a spot of pie, at Chico's Bakery."

67

Aaron was not only youthful, Rebecca observed, but powerfully built and seemed strongly attracted to her. She had to admit she found him equally absorbing. Considering that they would be sharing a train over one night, his manner urged her to agree.

"All right. You can tell me where I can find a good hotel for tonight."

Seated at one of four small wrought-iron tables with marble tops, the two young people gazed at each other over cups of savory, steaming coffee. Rebecca had ordered a light, flaky Mexican pastry and, true to his word, Aaron had a thick slice of pie. Its contents had an odd purple-red cast. Rebecca looked at it quizzically.

"Gooseberries and cactus apple fruit," Aaron explained. "It sounds awful, but it's delicious. Now, what takes you to Flagstaff?"

Rebecca hesitated. To be frank, to state that she was hunting a man down to kill him, didn't sound like the sort of thing she should confide to a lawman whom she had known for only a quarter of an hour. Some peace officers she knew would wish her luck and send her on her way. Aaron might not. To lie would be equally risky, since he already said he would be taking the same train.

"I—ah—I'm looking for someone. A person I haven't seen in a long time."

"Anything difficult about it? Something a deputy U.S. marshal could help you take care of?"

He certainly staked out his territory well in advance, Rebecca considered. She decided to answer him lightly. "Oh, no. Nothing quite so perilous as that. Now, tell me, Aaron, have you been here long?"

His blush and boyish smile returned. "Even a newcomer can tell. I'm not brown enough to be of Mexican background."

"Oh, but you are," Rebecca blurted, gave a short, nervous laugh, and explained. "At least your hands and face are."

"I'll concede that. Even though I speak Spanish well

68

enough, I do it with a terrible accent; I'm from Kansas. My folks have a farm," he added, almost apologetically. "So no one is going to mistake me for a native of New Mexico. As to the rest of it, I've been a deputy marshal for three years, assigned here in Santa Fe. I live alone, since I'm too young to be married." He risked a tentative grin. "Since you, too, are alone in a strange town, might I offer to take you to dinner?"

Surprised, Rebecca lowered almond-shaped lids, the long black lashes brushing her high cheekbones. Surprised when she examined her feelings, she found the idea appealing. "You certainly may. And the answer is . . . yes."

They dined late, in the Mexican custom, at nine o'clock. Aaron picked a place famous for its *barbacoa* and *carnitas*. Inside the wide, curving arches of the restaurant, the air was redolent with the odor of chiles, garlic, and mingled spices. In a huge, walk-in fireplace a side of goat and a hind leg of beef turned on a spit tended by a small boy, while a large copper cauldron of melted lard bubbled as chunks of pork cooked in it. Mariachis played exuberantly among the tables, and low, flickering candlelight provided a romantic atmosphere. Their conversation remained light during the meal. By the time the flan, shimmering yellow custards, with rich caramel sauce, came to the table, talk had gotten around to the nature of lawlessness in the area Aaron policed.

"Several of the witnesses that I interviewed suggested some sort of gang activity. They felt the claim jumpers and men forcing people out of the Flagstaff area weren't independent groups of three to five, but part of a larger organization."

"Which reminds me," Rebecca surged into her principal interst. "Have you heard of Chris Starret?"

He most certainly had—by way of *Wanted* fliers from Texas, warnings from the Texas Rangers and rumbles out of Mexico. A nasty bit of business, Aaron Hawkins considered Chris Starret. What would a lovely young woman like Rebecca Caldwell want to know about Chris Starret? The question plagued him into asking a direct question.

"Do you have a particular reason for bringing up his name?" He watched shrewdly as she made her answer.

"I—ah—I heard rumors in Denver that he might be mixed up in the Indian trouble around Flagstaff. From what you said, and, ah," she continued improvising, "considering his reputation, I thought claim-jumping might be the sort of thing he would get involved in. Especially if he has a gang set up again."

"A notorious outlaw like that," Aaron mused aloud. "I certainly hope I don't have to go up against him out there."

"As you should," Rebecca confided. "He's . . . extremely dangerous."

Intrigued, and growing suspicious of his companion's *bona fides,* Aaron tried to draw Rebecca out, learn more of her relationship to Chris Starret. Contrarily she changed the subject and would not be induced to speak of Starret again. It only served to make Aaron Hawkins more skeptical of Rebecca's involvement. Chafing to learn more, Aaron walked her to her room at the hotel and received a quick, firm, and endearing peck on the cheek.

"I had a lovely time, dinner was remarkable, and I'll see you in the morning," Rebecca said in dismissal.

It only fueled Aaron's fires of doubt.

The next morning dawned to disaster and delay. At the Atchison Topeka and Santa Fe depot, Rebecca and Aaron discovered that there would not be a train west that day. A mountain thunderstorm had created a flash flood which had wiped out a small bridge and a quarter mile of track. It would take until the next day to complete repairs.

All reticence seemed to have evaporated as Rebecca whirled impulsively to Aaron and asked, "What shall we do today?" She fairly purred, Aaron noted.

"Oh, I think we'll figure out something," he said confidently. Smiling, he offered his elbow and they departed arm-in-arm.

Filled with confidence that he had an unimpeachable argument in favor of immediate military intervention, Big Mac Kellogg took his dead and seriously wounded employees into Flagstaff. There he paid a call on Lieutenant Colonel Jeremy Alford, at the small cantonment on the edge of town. The commanding officer invited Big Mac into his office and listened politely to what the lumberman had to say, frowning at the vivid descriptions of what happened during the Shoshone attack. He offered his visitor coffee and sat silent a long minute.

"Mr. Kellogg, we've been over this before. The army is busy with the Apache in the southern part of the territory. There are also Mexican bandits—they call themselves revolutionaries—to contend with. General Crook's headquarters has neither the men nor the time to send them to Flagstaff, outside of the small garrison already here." Alford paused again, selecting his words carefully.

"We have problems enough without adding a fight with the Shoshone. The area you're talking about is thirty miles north of here. The Shoshone come down there from the north only during the spring and summer, to hunt. They have been doing so for centuries. It seems to me that your presence there is what's causing the trouble."

"Now see here, Colonel," Big Mac blustered. "That's an odd attitude for an officer in the United States Army. Your job is to protect the citizens against Indian depredations. *I* am an American citizen, and I demand that protection for myself and my men."

Alford's attitude turned hard, and there was an icy edge to his words. "I sometimes wonder if we're citizens

71

of the same United States. You're not the first entre-preneur I've encountered who devised some means of getting the army to play at private security force for their enterprises. Unfortunately, too often they succeed in having their way." With sudden swiftness the colonel banged a fist on his desk top. "But you aren't, mister. The Shoshone were there long before you came, and the treaty says they have the right to be there now. Considering all the circumstances I've described to you so far, the way I see it, you have three choices.

"One, you can stay here, quit cutting trees on Shoshone land and precipitating retaliation, and live in peace. Or you can quit and get out now, while you're still alive and in good health."

"What's the third?" Big Mac sneered, his patience with the army's representative evaporated.

"You can stay here, keep cutting, and lose your hair," Alford enunciated slowly and clearly.

Unaccustomed to not getting his way, Big Mac let his temper flare to white-hot. He stood rapidly, with such force that he overturned his chair. "Thank you *very* much, Colonel. It has been an enlightening afternoon. Maybe I should get myself a breechcloth and moccasins and let my hair grow long. Then you might listen to me with a little more sympathy."

When Big Mac Kellogg stomped out the door with a muttered "Goddamned Injun-lovers," it brought a crooked smile to Jeremy Alford's lips. A good officer, Alford didn't fail to make a note to keep an eye on Kellogg and be ready for the trouble he might cause.

A block away, in the largest saloon in Flagstaff, Big Mac Kellogg unloaded his misery and frustration on Chris Starret. Chris sipped from his glass of fine Tennessee whiskey and ran a hand over his glossy bald pate. Nodding, he pointed to a table. Once seated, he spoke to Kellogg with quiet earnestness.

"I see no real problem here, Mac. Give me a free hand, and a fifty-fifty partnership," Chris promised assuringly,

72

"and I'll rid the area of the Shoshone and the Utes. No Indians, no Indian troubles."

Aaron Hawkins had a glum expression when shortly before noon Rebecca Caldwell entered his tiny office in an annex of the courthouse—the former Governor-General's palace—on the main plaza in Santa Fe. Through the previous night he had pondered the incongruity of a pretty young woman asking questions about a dangerous and notorious outlaw like Chris Starret. After a restless night and hasty shave, Aaron had delayed calling for Rebecca to escort her to their expected departure. When they learned of the change of schedule, he had at first been delighted by the prospect of keeping company with the lovely Rebecca for another day in Santa Fe. Then, after they had breakfasted, he excused himself and returned to his small cubicle to sift through his desk and the four-drawer wooden file cabinet for all he had on Starret. After he read it through, Aaron reluctantly came to a conclusion regarding Rebecca—an erroneous one, yet the only one he could formulate, given the information at hand. She noticed at once his altered mood.

"Aaron, you look rather troubled," Rebecca observed. "Has something gone wrong?"

"In the face of destroying a pleasant acquaintanceship, Miss Caldwell, I'm afraid I have to ask you some serious and official questions."

Immediately cautious, Rebecca sought to defuse the situation. "My, my, so formal, Aaron . . . what sort of questions do you mean?"

Fighting to ignore the overpowering allure of her loveliness, Aaron stuck strictly to business. "About you and your relationship with one Christopher Starret, fugitive and outlaw."

"Oh, dear," Rebecca blurted before her ingrained self-control could prevent it. A tiny frown creased her high, smooth brow. "I can tell you truthfully, Aaron, that there's no, ah, 'relationship' between Chris Starret and myself."

Aaron wanted to believe her. He ached with the need to clear her of any of the ugly suspicions her remarks the previous night had kindled in him. "You seemed quite anxious to determine if Chris Starret figured into my going to Flagstaff. Could it be that you were concerned for his safety?"

Hurt put vertical creases at the inner edges of her arched, ebon eyebrows. Mentally caught up to the direction of this informal interrogation, Rebecca sought some means of satisfying Aaron while not revealing the entire story behind her interest in Starret.

"Believe me, the last thing I'm concerned for is his safety. I'd prefer to see him on the gallows," Rebecca added with considerable heat.

Aaron cocked one eyebrow. "Why's that?" he asked curtly.

"He—he murdered a man I cared about a great deal. Killed a lot of people I knew and liked. Aaron, I'm going to Flagstaff because of the Indian troubles with a logging company. It's as simple as that. I'm not connected to the government, to the Bureau of Indian Affairs. I'm doing it because I have a degree of influence with some of the tribes."

Averse to relenting too easily, Aaron probed further with a bluntness that edged on rudeness. "Go on."

"Well, ah, you see, I'm, ah, I was at one time a captive of the Sioux. The *Tísayaota* Oglala band. I don't want to go into all of that, it's the past and done. I'm trying to bring peace. I was only worried that Chris Starret might be mixed up in the unrest among the Shoshone. He's done that sort of thing before."

Aaron frowned. "You know, in some areas you could be held as a material witness. You could be put in jail for that until you came up with everything you know about Starret. There are also territorial laws about civilians having dealings with the various tribes. In Arizona Territory you could be locked up for a long time if you got caught at it. But frankly, Rebecca, I don't really give a damn," he concluded warmly, flashing his usual smile and radiating his repressed feelings for the lovely white squaw.

"Then you *do* believe me?" Rebecca gusted, brightening.

"I . . . let's say that I *prefer* to accept your version of these, ah, unusual circumstances. I always have," he added with a gulp.

"It's a long story, and terribly involved. I'd rather not have to go into every detail. If you wish to verify my interest in the Shoshone difficulties, you can telegraph to Lieutenant Arthur Trapp, United States Army Department of the Platte, Standing Rock Outpost, Wyoming Territory."

"No. I'd rather have you tell me a little more of it over dinner tonight. After all, we depart for Flagstaff tomorrow at noon, and we should celebrate."

Chapter 8

Rebecca Caldwell looked out from under the tassled fringe of the sprightly surrey that Aaron Hawkins drove with consummate skill. They rattled along a well-maintained road toward the large ranch of Don Hernan Soto y Melendres, where they had been invited for a late dinner and *baile* to follow. Roadrunners paced the vehicle, while an early nighthawk orbited above, seeking its prey. During the day, at Aaron's insistence, Rebecca had acquired several items of outdoor clothing he suggested would be useful around Flagstaff. They had encountered Don Hernan at the entrance to a large, busy restaurant on the plaza at noontime. Delighted that the deputy had not departed, the grandee had tendered his invitation at once.

Pleased to be included in the invitation, Rebecca spent the afternoon making ready for the excursion. With an hour of strong southwest sunlight remaining, Aaron advised her that they had only a mile left to travel. Rebecca decided to bring the conversation around to her pressing interest.

"Tell me about Flagstaff," she encouraged.

"It's a new town, not large as yet. Raw, with a lot of buildings not even painted," he began. "There's plenty of the rough element there, as can be expected in such a community."

"There's considerable lawlessness there?" Rebecca probed.

"Not really," Aaron allowed. "At least, nothing out of the ordinary. The city fathers mentioned in their letter to me that we might appoint a town marshal while I'm there investigating the killings. So it sounds like law and order are on the way."

"If Flagstaff is wide open at present, it might be Chris Starret has set up there and no one's aware of it," Rebecca prompted.

Aaron frowned. Her words had awakened his earlier, uneasy train of thought. He had no time to contemplate it, for he looked away from his lovely companion to find four squat, ugly men in sombreros and sarapes blocking the trail. They did not openly display their firearms, but sat their scrawny mounts with nasty expressions on their unshaven faces. Obsidian eyes burned with a barely suppressed hatred of gringos. Drooping, raven-hued mustaches circled their mouths. The one in the middle raised his hand to signal a halt. His mouth formed a round, open pucker before he spoke.

"Ramon, wha' have we heer? Two gringos on their way to Don Hernan's fiesta, no? Well, gringos, you are in the presence of four poor sons of Mexico who seek to correct the inequities that made our lowly station. We wish to redistribute the wealth that has been denied us. That is only fair, ¿como no? So, señor y señorita, we begin with you. Please remove all of your valuables and hand them to my assistant."

"You've picked the wrong people to rob," Aaron stated with menace. "I'm a deputy United States marshal." He tugged at the left side of his coat to reveal the badge on his vest. It also distracted the attention of the bandits while he dropped his right hand to the butt-stock of his .45 Colt.

"And I am *el Lobo Loco*. Even this far north, men hear my name and tremble. Do as I say," he snarled.

"I suppose we haven't any choice," Rebecca directed

to Aaron as she kept her gaze fixed on the outlaw to the leader's left.

Smiling, she reached into her ample handbag. "Do it now, Aaron," she said tightly, her hand steady on the .38 Smith & Wesson Baby Russian which she fired twice through the bottom of her purse an instant later. The bullets struck the fat bandito next to *el Lobo Loco* in the chest. The bandit grunted with each impact and sagged in his saddle. By then, Aaron had his sixgun out and fired at point-blank range into the surprised face of *el Lobo Loco*.

Rebecca brought the smoking revolver from her bag and triggered another round at the outlaw on the far right, grazing his neck. He wailed in agony and clapped a hand to the wound. The reins released, his horse shied at the bitter copper smell of blood and the violent noise of discharging firearms. Crowhopping, it carried the wounded bandito away from the smoke-hazed scene.

Aaron shot another of the robbers, seriously wounding him in the abdomen. Rising, he threw a shot at the fleeing outlaw which had no effect. Then Aaron dismounted from the surrey and disarmed the wounded bandit. He made a check of the dead men and looked back at Rebecca, who also stood, her small pocket gun trained on the would-be stick-up men. Curiosity and new suspicions welled up in Aaron as he digested what had happened in the brief seconds of the shootout. She had calmly and deliberately shot two men, killing one, with a respectable sized hideout gun and seemed not the least disturbed by the action.

"My God, Miss Rebecca," he stammered. "Wh—what possessed you to do that?"

"I didn't want to be robbed. And I didn't think you did, either," she stated calmly.

"You . . . sure know how to handle a gun."

"I've had . . . some practice, Aaron."

Aaron swallowed hard, as though to choke down the bevy of questions that welled up, demanding answers. "We'll take these men in to Don Hernan's. His *mayoral*

79

will notify the local law. I'm sorry this happened to spoil our evening."

"It needn't," Rebecca answered cool and collected, "if you don't want it to."

Little of the fading twilight seeped in through the cracks in the stout shed at the sawmill, where White Rabbit and Sweet Grass lay as captives. Although given only a small bucket of water and a single meal daily, they fared rather well. White Rabbit's wound had closed and scabbed over and now itched furiously as a sign of its healing. That there was only a slight puckered redness around the entrance and exit points could be considered a good sign. His strength had returned also.

"Will they hit us again?" Sweet Grass asked of his little friend.

"That was because the warriors came," White Rabbit explained. "The white-eyes were angry and took it out on us."

"They wanted to know where the main camp was. I didn't tell them," Sweet Grass added proudly.

"Nor I," White Rabbit affirmed. "If the men come again to fight, the white-eyes will be mean to us and hurt us more. We must leave this place. We can find our way home."

"How can we do it? The door will not move unless a white-eye does something with it." Sweet Grass didn't understand locks.

"This strange lodge rests on the ground, like those of our people," White Rabbit began unveiling a plan he had considered in the hours while he lay recovering from his wound. "We can dig under it and crawl out. It would be best to do at night."

"What do we dig with?"

White Rabbit wrinkled his brow. "I'm—not sure. If we could keep the metal dishes our food comes in . . ." he grew silent in speculation.

"I know how we can do that," Sweet Grass announced cheerfully. "We can eat slowly, and then beg to keep our dishes until we're done. The brown-skinned one is not an enemy. He is kind and I think would help us if he could."

Thinking that over, White Rabbit shifted on his rude bed of pine boughs. "We can try it, we can see. We must get away before they do worse things to us."

After an uneventful ride back into Santa Fe, following dinner and dancing at Don Hernan Soto's, Rebecca invited Aaron to her room when they reached her hotel. With the impish smile of a small boy indulging in a forbidden pleasure, Aaron accepted and produced a bottle of champagne from a cloth bundle he had sequestered in the surrey.

"You took quite a bit for granted, believing I would ask you in," Rebecca accused.

"I *hoped* you might. It was worth the risk and . . . I could always drink the champagne alone," Aaron answered lightly.

Rebecca removed her light wrap and took Aaron's hat. The young lawman took charge of the wine, popping the cork and pouring into two thick, barrel hotel glasses. He handed one to Rebecca and set the bottle, a magnum, aside.

"Here's to a pleasant journey. *Feliz viaje.*"

"To that . . . and to a pleasant night," Rebecca added with a long, sultry look.

They downed the bubbling wine and Aaron poured more. He lifted his in another toast. "To a beautiful woman."

Flushing lightly, Rebecca drank deeply. Smiling, her deep blue eyes sparkling, she took a step toward him. Aaron plucked the glass from her hand and put aside his own. He closed the space between them and Rebecca came into his arms. They embraced. Amid whispered protests of surprise and joy, Aaron kissed her face lightly,

81

eyelids, cheeks, nose, forehead, chin and jawline.

"Oh, Rebecca . . ." kiss "I never . . ." kiss "expected anything . . ." kiss "like this . . ." kiss. His fluttering lips found hers and he intensified the ardor of his kisses.

Her lips parted under his insistent pressure, then her teeth. Like a shaft of fire, his tongue entered her mouth. With amorous determination he explored that cavity with a thoroughness that left them both breathless. When he made to withdraw and regain his composure, Rebecca's tongue followed his, seeking the secrets she could find behind his lips. With the long, strong fingers of one hand, Aaron cupped and squeezed Rebecca's right breast. She murmured her approval against the pressure of their erotic kiss.

Rebecca clung to him, arms entwined around his neck, one leg bent up at the knee, the other spread wide so that she could grind her pubic mound against the long, rigid presence behind his trouser fly. Aaron's other hand, at the small of her back, went to her buttocks and shoved her against his throbbing erection with greater effort.

She groaned and tried to speak, but Aaron's insistent tongue thrust into her mouth again. Shivering with a rising frenzy, Rebecca began to churn against his bulging phallus. Tiny beads of passion's dew formed on her forehead. Her heart pounded in her chest and a dizziness of euphoria swept through her consciousness. All too soon their embrace ended.

Even then they continued to touch, to stroke each other, and Rebecca kept her pubis tightly clamped against the blatantly solid evidence of his arousal. Aaron kissed the hollow of her throat, worked upward to her chin, along one jawline. His tongue found the curlicues of one ear. Rebecca sighed and breathed in harsh, audible gasps. She placed one hand between them and clamped her fingers over his heated member. Aaron came to her lips again and locked her in a monumental blending of their flesh.

Little squeaks and moans of ecstacy came from deep in

Rebecca's throat. At last she broke away and spoke with a tone of urgency. "Oh, God, hurry Aaron. Undress me, hurry."

His big, thick, callused fingers became nimble in the pursuit of unfastening the many buttons of Rebecca's dress. Slowly he peeled her out of it and let the taffeta and silk creation sink to the floor. Rebecca stepped out of it, and Aaron knelt to undo her shoe bindings. Her well-formed feet, somewhat wide at the front from years of going barefoot and wearing moccasins, came free, and Aaron slid down her stockings. Her petticoats rustled as he undid the fastenings and let them drop.

"Oh, Aaron, I—I want you so badly," Rebecca gasped. She clutched at him, drawing him to her embrace. Again their lips met and parted, their tongues explored and savored.

Rebecca ground against his rigid phallus, thrilling at its closeness with only his garments and her under-drawers separating her from it. She began to work his shirt buttons. Aaron cupped her breasts and squeezed them gently, thumbs manipulating her stiffening nipples and drew them out to full length. Rebecca moaned and pulled his shirt free. Their bare skin touched. They recoiled from the overload of delightful sensation it produced, then clasped tightly once again.

While they kissed, Rebecca used one hand to fumble with Aaron's belt, the other grasped his pulsing manhood. She rushed to rid him of the last of his clothing and pushed back to inspect his manly figure. Muscles bulged on shoulders, arms and chest. Ridges on his flat belly highlighted its trim nature. Curving upward from a nest of brown strands, his stone-hard penis swayed with each tiny motion of his hips.

"Oooh, it's wonderful, Aaron, wonderful," Rebecca cooed as she wrapped capable fingers around his shaft and began slowly to stroke the loose outer sheath.

"Ummmm. Seems you've done this a bit before."

"Oh, a few times," Rebecca said lightly.

"If it's up to me, you can keep it up a long, long time."

"If you can keep it up, I can keep it going," she answered bawdily.

Aaron directed one hand to her nearly hairless mound. His fingers searched and probed, entering her hot, moist cleft. There they sped to the center of her excitation and began to tease the sensitive length of flesh, setting off a shower of exquisite sensations.

Rebecca heaved against his probing grasp, exciting herself more. Their kiss ended with both breathless. Rebecca began to lick and nibble at Aaron's face, ears, neck, and chest. Her head bowed and she covered one, then the other nipple with passionate osculation. His contact broke with her hot, slippery interior as she sank to her knees.

Leaving a long trail of fire, her tongue slid down his hard body, found the firm squiggle of his navel. Circling it in a tantalizing way, she continued downward. Making wide, delightful arcs across his pubic arch, she approached the small, thick thatch of curly brown hair at the base of his swollen organ. Her hand barely encompassed it, and she increased the speed of her strokes as she closed in on the large, firm sack suspended below.

Lipping his stones and darting her tongue to the underside of his long, curved staff, she worked outward from his body. Aaron made soft, whuffling sounds as she reached the sensitive tip, wet it and began to describe spirals across the short, blunt surface. Aaron shivered and placed a hand behind her head, encouraging further exploration. Opening wide, Rebecca indulged him.

"Aaaah, mighty fine," Aaron sighed out.

Tightening her lips around the stout barrel of his manly weapon, Rebecca began to pump it with hungry urgency. Her own arousal made her nearly frantic with a desperate need to consume all of him. She tried. Eyes open to appreciate the great shaft sliding back and forth, she strove mightily to swallow Aaron to the hilt. It seemed she would be blessed with success, when the turmoil of her great need overwhelmed her determination. Expelling his rigid member she rose up, pleading.

"Take me, Aaron, oh, hurry, take me now."

Aaron lifted her light frame and carried her to the bed. Cooing to her, he gently spread her legs and knelt between them. His big hands stroked the inside of her thighs as he moved closer. His nearly hairless body felt silken against her flesh. Eagerly she reached out and guided his prize to the wet and welcoming sheath that awaited it. With a foreshortened thrust of his lean hips, Aaron entered her. He made only a hand's width of penetration when she cried out euphorically.

"*Aaaüiieeee, Aaaaarooon.* More, make me quiver. *Aaaaah, Aaaarrrronnn.*"

Swiftly, then, he hilted her, driving his tingling projection deep into the core of her soft, moist, fiery passage. Waves of contractions thrilled them both. With studied care he began to piston his hips, rocking the both of them as the bed creaked and groaned. Tossing her head from side to side, Rebecca bit her lip. Oh, my, what a wonderful way to end the day, she mused as her emotions whirled. If only it could go on until morning's first light.

Aaron proved strong in the long stretch. His passion slaked once, he never even paused before grinding them toward another magnificent completion. Untiringly he vied with her to invent new and more satisfying manners of coupling, until the cock crowed in a distant yard and a thin bar of steely gray divided earth from sky along the eastern horizon.

"I hope . . . with all my heart . . . that we'll have a chance . . . to repeat this before we reach . . . Flagstaff," Rebecca panted out as she surrendered to well-deserved slumber for two scant hours.

Chapter 9

With a loud, nimble-footed clatter, Rebecca Caldwell's Palouse stallion, *Sila*, climbed the loading ramp and let himself be led to a tether ring at the rear, right sidewall of the car. A single pole at shoulder height served as a token stall. Aaron's line-back sorrel went in next. Satisfied with the disposition of their animals, Rebecca and Aaron sought out their seats in one of the two first-class Pullman cars. No sooner they had seated themselves than Aaron voiced an unexpected concern.

"This is the first time I've used the train for rapid transport. I'm concerned about Buck. Do horses travel well in those drafty cars?"

"I've never had any problems, even on the Mexican railway system," Rebecca reassured him. "Oh, on long journeys horses will grow a little stiff-legged, and they often have trouble readjusting to solid ground after the rocking and swaying of the cars. But that's only for minutes, an hour at most."

"Well," Aaron began reluctantly. "If you say so."

A screech of metal and a sudden lurch of the car proclaimed the beginning of their journey. The shrill whistle of the locomotive hooted its message and the big drivers spun again, couplings taking on the strain in earnest. Another blast from the steam whistle—one long and three shorts—and the outskirts of Santa Fe slid past the windows, giving way to the reds, browns, and oranges of the high-altitude desert. Cacti in confusing variety dotted the rocks and sand. An accomplished train rider, Rebecca found the gentle rocking of the coach gently lulled her into a drowsy state.

"You're falling asleep," Aaron intruded on her fleeing consciousness.

"After last night, it seems a good idea," Rebecca teased, remembering their joyful allaying of Aaron's suspicions.

"Should we have the porter make up a Pullman berth for us?" Aaron suggested.

"Now? In broad daylight?" Rebecca squeaked. "We'd scandalize all these good people."

"Better now than when they're trying to sleep. You're, ah, rather vocal in your appreciation of good loving."

"*Aaron!*" Rebecca wailed, embarrassed. "Let's talk about something else."

Eyes twinkling, Aaron put a hand lightly on her arm. "Am I reaching you?"

"Yes," Rebecca admitted miserably.

Quietly he inserted a gentle probe. "Then why don't you tell me more about you and what Chris Starret did?"

"Why, I already told you." She frowned, relented. "All right. He betrayed Roger Styles into my hands, in return for his freedom. By itself, that doesn't bother me at all. Then he broke his word to leave Texas and began robbing and pillaging, eventually killed the man I loved very much, and nearly finished me off. Since then he's stirred up trouble between the northern Shoshone and the Arapaho, conducted a land swindle, and been responsible for at least twenty murders. The thought of him being mixed up in something in Flagstaff worries me."

Aaron chuckled indulgently. "After the way you handled those banditos the other night? Not likely," Aaron answered his rhetorical question. "Why is it I get the feeling you're interested in these Indian problems because you think Starret is mixed up in it and you might get a shot at him?"

Cornered, Rebecca sought to fall back. Lowering her long, ebon lashes in a coy manner, she cooed, "Let's talk about making love, shall we?"

Three hours out from Santa Fe, the AT&SF Daylight slowed and pulled onto a siding to take on water and await a meet with the eastbound express. A portly conductor walked through the cars announcing the stop.

"Water stop, folks. We'll be here about an hour, till the express goes through. Y'can get out and stretch your legs. Whistle'll call you back in good time. Shelter house over there, some Mezkin ladies who sell tamales and burritos, and an enterprising feller with cold beer, sarsparilla, an' root beer."

"Shall we?" Rebecca prompted. "I love tamales and I could sure use a cold beer to wash them down."

"Good thinking. They'll be fiery hot in this country," Aaron informed her. "Then maybe we can take a little walk?"

"Any special reason for a stroll?" Rebecca queried.

In the same manner as he had done when they learned of the delay in their train, Aaron produced an impish expression and repeated his reply. "We'll think of something."

They had little trouble doing that. After consuming half a dozen small, succulent tamales each, washed down with cool—if not cold—beer, Aaron led Rebecca off into the mesquite, silver bush and palo verde and down a slight incline. Out of sight of the Daylight and its passengers, they embraced. Aaron kissed with an ardor undiminished by their amorous night. Rebecca responded eagerly.

"We, ah, really haven't time to properly consummate this moment of privacy," Aaron told her after their kiss ended.

"No, that's true," Rebecca acknowledged, one hand on his firm manhood. "And hardly the proper accommodations. But . . . I do . . . have one idea."

Hoisting the skirt of her traveling dress, Rebecca sank to her knees before him. Deftly she opened his fly and brought his rigid phallus out into the sun-bright desert air. Aaron sighed and watched fondly while she manipulated it, feathery light strokes mingled with tantalizing flicks of her tongue and teasing flutter of heavenly lips. He put one large hand on top of her head.

"How does a woman . . . manage to take pleasure from this?" he asked in a hoarse whisper.

"Oh, I do, Aaron. You can believe me I do," Rebecca assured him.

Sighing in happy abandon, Aaron surrendered himself to Eros as Rebecca opened wide and took what she could of his throbbing member deep into her mouth, her lips and tongue performing miracles of delight while she tugged demandingly at his bulk. On she went, drawing him up the long slope toward a tremendous crescendo.

Shortly before the ultimate moment, Rebecca began to moan. Abruptly she stood up and hoisted high her voluminous skirts. "Oh, Aaron, I can't stand it any longer. Take me, here, now, standing up. Oh, hurry, dearest."

Startled, Aaron nevertheless complied exuberantly. Lifting her so she rode his hips, legs twined around him, he entered her fevered cleft and drove toward her soul. Rebecca shivered and helped as best she could. Burning with the tumultuous burst of sensation, they ground toward a new euphoria.

Stroke after stroke brought little cheeps and moans of happiness from Rebecca. Clinging tightly to Aaron's broad shoulders, she made tight, circular motions with her buttocks, adding new dimension to the smooth, gliding thrusts of his magnificent maleness. All too soon, thanks to her earlier determined attention, Aaron raced to the brink and cascaded over. Stifling a howl of release, Rebecca swiftly joined him.

Trembling, their contractions and convulsions decreased into the genial peace of the afterglow. A strident shriek from the Baldwin locomotive's steam whistle jerked them back to the urgency of the present.

"Oh, my, I think that was marvelous," Rebecca panted as they disengaged and rearranged their clothing.

"We'll have to hurry, or we'll have a long walk," Aaron urged.

"Right now I wouldn't even care. We'd have more time for . . . for that."

"Woman, you are insatiable."

"I surely hope so," Rebecca teased. "Now, we've got a train to catch."

It had been a painful lesson for Big Mac Kellogg. Not that he had endured physical harm or intimidation. No, Chris Starret didn't work that way. It was a blow to Kellogg's self-esteem to have to admit that the brutal, bloodthirsty suggestions Starret made offered the only way to achieve what he wanted. To apply that solution, Starret wanted an equal partnership. That had galled Big Mac most of all. In the end, after a week's consideration, he agreed.

"Good," Chris Starret stated simply. "We can get going."

"How do you propose to handle it? Between us we don't have enough men to take on the whole Shoshone tribe."

"One thing at a time, Mac," Chris said easily. "I am setting up Duffey and Grayson to help me recruit a large force of eager Indian fighters. We'll pick drifters and unemployed gunhands for the most part. With a few local fellows, my men and Aaron to fill in the leadership, I've got twenty-five gunnies you've never seen in camp not two hours' ride from here."

Stunned by this revelation, Big Mac sat back in his chair and gripped the arms tightly. "Why wasn't I told of this? There could have been trouble between my boys and yours."

"Relax. There was none, and they're ours now," Chris assured him. "Once we have seventy-five, eighty, we track down those Shoshone and wipe them out."

"It would be easier finding out from those kids where the village is located," Mac suggested.

Chris raised a thin eyebrow. Furrows wrinkled his bald pate, and his gray eyes turned hard and cold. "You still have them around? I thought you'd have gotten rid of them after that Indian attack."

"They're—ah—only kids," Big Mac pleaded.

"You heard what Bill Sherman said about that. 'Nits make lice.' Well, if you haven't eliminated them yet, have someone bring them here and we'll see what we can learn."

Eyes wide with fright, though they struggled to keep their faces blank and impassive, White Rabbit and Sweet Grass had themselves dragged into the presence of two obviously important white men. The one White Rabbit sensed to be younger, though he had no hair, spoke to them in the white tongue. His words meant nothing. White Rabbit shrugged and replied with his name in Shoshone.

Quick as a striking snake, the big white man lashed out and struck the boy with a powerful backhand blow. It knocked White Rabbit off his feet and slammed him against a heavy wooden chair. The wound in his side throbbed with new pain.

"God damn it, speak English," Chris Starret snarled.

"Not know, not know," White Rabbit peeped, fighting back tears.

Chris snatched a burning cigarette from John Duffey's fingers and drove the glowing red coal against the youngster's right biceps. Unable to prevent it, White Rabbit let a scream rip from his throat. Big, hot tears ran down his cheeks.

"Not know." It was a choked whisper.

Chris turned to the other Indian boy. "You, Injun

brat, where is your village?"

Sweet Grass shook his head in confusion and muttered in Shoshone. Starret rammed a big hand into his belly, right below the rib cage, and Sweet Grass thought for a moment his heart would be crushed. The agony he felt nearly made him lose consciousness. Gasping, he again pleaded that he did not understand.

"I'm going to get something out of you two, or else," Chris growled.

"Chris," Big Mac said softly, earnestly. "I don't think they understand you. I don't think they speak any English."

Chris took time to light a cigar. When he had it glowing well, he pressed it against Sweet Grass' chest. The little lad shrieked in agony. "Then we'll teach it to 'em."

"You can't do that. At least not the way you're trying," Kellogg objected. "You'll kill them before they can say good morning."

"Then get someone in here who speaks that savage gabble of theirs," Chris demanded.

"I don't know if there's anyone in camp who can," Big Mac complained. "I'll go and see."

While he sought out someone who could speak Shoshone, Chris amused himself tormenting the children. He burned both boys liberally with his cigar. Laughing maniacally, he squeezed their testicles in a powerful hand to the point of nearly crushing them. White Rabbit, who was nearer puberty than his friend, suffered immensely and passed out. A splash of water revived him.

"You're gonna talk, boy. You'll tell me everything I want to know," Chris crooned to him.

His doubled fist smashed into White Rabbit's bare ribs. One bone made a crack like a .22 shot, and White Rabbit doubled up on the floor, hugging himself and rocking in new misery. Sweet Grass suddenly found his courage and attacked Chris, small fists slamming the tall, lean outlaw in the lower abdomen. Chris snatched him

93

off his feet and hurled the Shoshone boy to the floor. Sweet Grass lay there, stunned and vulnerable.

Chris raised a booted foot to stomp the child's belly when Big Mac returned with Lupe Bargas, the camp cook. "What the hell!" Big Mac exploded. "You leave them alone or you'll not get a word out of them."

Ignoring Bic Mac, Chris turned to the cook. "Well, Lupe, can you talk Shoshone?"

"Sí. A little, Señor Chris," Lupe acknowledged, hat clutched in both hands in front of his chest in the presence of the patron.

"Ask them where their village is."

Lupe rattled off a sentence in Shoshone. Softly sobbing from their injuries, neither boy said anything in return. Lupe tried again. Still nothing.

"Get a pair of pliers," Chris commanded.

John Duffey left to do his boss' bidding. Chris turned back to the Indian children and his translator. "Tell them that I'm going to start on their fingers, then their toes. If they don't talk, I'll use the pliers on their balls."

With a sick expression that implied the threats had been made to him, Lupe complied. Sweet Grass muttered a soft response.

"What is that, *niño?*" Lupe asked in a kindly tone, bent low.

"Why has he hurt us?" Sweet Grass repeated louder.

"The big one with no hair wants you to tell him where your village is located."

"It will have moved. When the warriors attacked here, they would not have gone to the new village. The people will hide now."

"Yes—yes, I know. Just . . . tell him anything. Send them off anywhere."

"Enough," Chris roared as Duffey returned.

He grabbed the tool from Duffey's hand and took hold of Sweet Grass's left hand. The jaws of the plier opened and Chris selected the little finger. He placed the first joint of Sweet Grass's pinky against the lower teeth and

94

began to close the tool. Sweet Grass wriggled in his grasp, unable to tear his gaze away from the terrible instrument that was about to ruin his finger. Stoically Sweet Grass bit his lower lip and vowed silently not to cry out at the pain.

It came in such intensity that he had no control over the raw, horrifying noise that erupted from his mouth as the plier bit into flesh and blood began to squirt. His body convulsed in agony and he shrieked over and over when the bone made a ghastly sound as Chris pulverized it. Then, mercifully, he passed out.

"Gimme the other one," Chris commanded.

"No! No, I'll tell you," White Rabbit pleaded as Duffey dragged him forward to receive the same torture. Lupe translated.

"All right, where is that village."

Sobbing, his words panted out over the dizzy waves of pain that tormented his body, White Rabbit described the trails to take, the landmarks to guide by to find their village. He knew, like Sweet Grass, that the people would have moved before the attack on the camp. He didn't care. He had to do something to stop the horrid pain. Suddenly stricken with gagging sickness, White Rabbit vomited weakly onto the floor.

"You little bastard," Chris swore. He reached for a finger with his plier. "I'm gonna take a finger just to make sure."

"No," Big Mac boomed. "You've done enough—too much. Can't you see the kid's beyond being clever or cooking up a lie? He's told you all he knows."

"How many warriors in the village?" Chris snapped, yanking White Rabbit's head up by one braid.

"T-t-two hands of five," the demolished boy blurted.

"Fifty," Lupe translated.

"How many more could that chief of yours count on for help?"

"I—I—I don't know."

Chris backhanded him again. "He's telling the truth!"

Lupe objected.

"How can you be sure?" Chris challenged.

Lupe shrugged. "Put yourself in his place. If all that has been done to him had been done to you as a little boy, would you have been able to make up fancy lies to fool grown men?"

"No. I suppose not," Chris grudgingly allowed.

"Then end this pointless, unmerciful torment, Señor Chris. *Por amor del dios.*"

"For the love of God, Lupe?" Chris taunted. "You going soft on us?"

Holding the trembling boy close against his chest, Lupe looked up with an expression of black hatred. "When it comes to torturing little children I am. I am a cook, Señor Chris, not a butcher *ladrón.*"

"I agree with Lupe," Big Mac growled, flexing his huge fists and bulging forearms.

Thwarted, Chris looked from one opponent to the other and back at the boys. "Get 'em outa here," he growled in resignation.

Chapter 10

His finger throbbed and sent out waves of joint-aching agony. It had swelled to the size of a cow's udder. Sweet Grass had become convinced it would split open from the pressure. He fought a desperate battle to keep from crying again. Huddled together with White Rabbit against the chill of the night, he knew he could endure no more torment. What would happen when the evil whites went to the old campsite and found the village moved? Surely they would come back and hurt him again. Unable to endure more, Sweet Grass made his decision.

"We have to do it tonight," he whispered close to White Rabbit's ear. "We can finish digging our hole and slip through."

"I hurt so badly," White Rabbit protested. "I can hardly move. I—I thought he would twist my balls off."

"Mine are swelled up big as a grown man's. But we've got to leave here right now. Please, help me dig."

Twenty minutes of diligent scraping opened the hole under the foundationless shack to an extent that Sweet Grass could wriggle through with some effort. White Rabbit tried it and found it too tight. He motioned to his friend.

"Go on, get in the shadows. I have to go back inside and dig some more."

When he tried, White Rabbit found he could not

move. The cord of his breechcloth had snagged on some sort of protruberance and imprisoned him half inside and half outside the improvised jail. He tried to slide a hand in at his side and feel around. His attempt failed. He could not force his hand past his own skin. Some three or four inches of solid wood made a barrier between his questing fingers and the object that held him fast. He wiggled, thrashed, and flailed to no benefit.

"Be quiet," Sweet Grass commanded in a harsh whisper. "The white-eyes will hear."

"I'm caught! Go on. Run while you can. I can't go in or out. Go, Sweet Grass and tell my grandfather of what has happened to me. Hurry!"

"But I don't . . ." Sweet Grass started.

"Run. Go now, or you will be caught," White Rabbit urged, on the edge of weeping in frustration.

"I—I'm going," Sweet Grass responded sadly.

Then silence filled the night. Slowly White Rabbit let his head droop onto one folded arm, and the tears of defeat and terror spilled onto the ground. He won control of his jumbled emotions after a while and tried again to free himself. His efforts proved to be of no avail. At last fatigue sneaked in and smothered him in sleep.

White Rabbit awakened to the hot fire of terrible new pain. Someone had grabbed him by the shoulders and yanked hard enough to break the cord of his breechcloth. It left a red welt around his hips and a long, copiously bleeding gash along his leg. When his wild eyes focused, he saw that the hairless one held him in huge hands, shaking him until his vision blurred again.

"Where is he? Where is that redskin bastard? Answer me," Chris Starret screamed at him.

New pains came as he was thrown to the ground. "Take him and do anything you need to make him talk," Chris ordered. "Have Lupe translate."

White Rabbit's screams began within fifteen minutes. They went on for a long while, during which Chris Starret had three cups of coffee, ate a hearty breakfast and made ready to ride into Flagstaff. The child's wails of agony cut off abruptly and John Duffey came to where Chris stood beside his horse.

"The boys got a little carried away, Chris. The kid's dead."

"No matter. But we'll have to move faster against the Shoshone. Come into town with me and we'll start recruitin' men."

"We'll be there tomorrow," Rebecca Caldwell observed while the desert terrain dwindled and lush, dark green conifers, aspen, and burr oak grew in number.

The train slowed to nearly a walking pace as the incline increased west of Navajo, Arizona Territory. To the north and south of the AT&SF tracks lay a fascinating, yet puzzling display of nature, the Petrified Forest. Inside their coach no one felt the gradual drop in temperature as the altitude rose.

"And then what?" Aaron asked with a note of caution.

Rebecca shrugged. "You look for your killers and I try to contact the Shoshone."

Despite their intimacy, or perhaps because of it, Aaron could not avoid the question he next posed. "And what about Chris Starret?"

"We don't even know if he is anywhere around Flagstaff," Rebecca snapped, ire raised defensively for a moment. Then she smiled and patted Aaron's arm to modify her reaction. "If he is and you find him, put him in jail. He's wanted in a lot of places."

"What if you find him first?" Aaron pressed.

A slight frown disturbed Rebecca's brow. She didn't want to lie outright to Aaron. They had become too close for that. Yet she didn't have any desire to come out and admit her purpose in coming to Flagstaff. Carefully she chose her reply.

"If Chris Starret comes up in connection with the Indian unrest, I promise I'll let you know."

Apparently mollified by that, Aaron changed the subject. "That's a good hundred fifty miles down the tracks, so what about something more immediate? What do we do with tonight?"

Rebecca produced a coy smile of infinite promise. "I'm . . . working on a surprise for you. Something I'm sure you'll like."

Rebecca's surprise came long after the other passengers had withdrawn to the dark privacy of their Pullman berths. She and Aaron had spent a long evening on the observation platform watching the stars and talking about matters trivial and complex, carefully avoiding any mention of Chris Starret. By then they were descending the western scarp of the short, buttonhook-shaped Rio Puerco range. Ahead of them lay Winslow, and beyond, Canyon Diablo and Walnut Creek Canyon. At last they reached Flagstaff, high in the forested mountains south of Humphries Peak, the highest point in Arizona Territory.

"Are you comfortable?" Aaron interrupted one of his stories about the northern Arizona country to inquire.

He had an arm around her shoulders, holding her possessively against his side. The movement of his breathing excited her as his chest expanded and his ribs slid against the side of her right breast. Suffused with a warm glow, Rebecca put her right arm around his waist.

"Yes, this shawl is enough for now," Rebecca assured him. Then she added coquettishly, "Besides, we'll be going in soon."

"Hmm. For what purpose, might I ask?" Aaron played along.

"Why, to go to sleep, of course. What else?" Rebecca teased.

"I, ah, thought you had a surprise for me." Aaron sounded a bit disappointed.

"Oh, I do, I do," Rebecca assured him as she released her arm and turned abruptly. She reached back and took his hand, leading him into the rear half of the last coach,

100

the smoking car.

In the next one forward, their Pullman bunks waited, ready and inviting. Rebecca put a finger to Aaron's lips, urging quiet, while she made signs with the other hand and arm that he was to get undressed in his bunk, then join her in hers. Aaron's eyes widened and he nodded enthusiastic agreement. Rebecca gave him a light peck on the cheek, and they parted company.

In less than three minutes, Aaron parted the curtain to her berth and climbed inside. He wore only the cut-off bottoms of a pair of red flannel longjohns. The garment readily revealed the state of his arousal. He found Rebecca naked and waiting for him. Hairless except for a sparse thatch along the centerline of his sternum, Aaron made silken contact with her passion-sensitized skin when they lay facing each other and embraced.

On their first wonderful night of loving, Rebecca had made comment on his lack of body hair, comparing his condition to Indian males. "Never had much," Aaron had confided. "Wearing long johns and rough clothes accounted for most of that." Rebecca asked what that had to do with it, to which he responded, "Wore it right off. Had some on my arms and legs when I was a little kid, fine as baby hair, but by the time I turned nineteen it had been rubbed plum off. Never came back." Now she rejoiced for its lack.

"Umm, you're so smooth," she murmured in Aaron's ear as she ran a hand across his chest.

"You're not bad yourself," he responded, duplicating her action, pausing long enough to firmly massage each nipple. "I—ah—like your choice in surprises."

"Thought you would. Hmm, what's this? It's poking away like a hungry piglet looking for the teat."

With her fingers firmly wrapped around his rigid phallus, Aaron began to nuzzle the hollow at the base of her throat. With practiced ease she slid him out of his "summarized" long johns and set about in earnest to give his stout member the best her hand could offer.

101

"I don't want this to sound like a complaint," Aaron teased, "but can't you find something better to do with that?"

Rebecca said nothing. She raised her upper leg and cocked it over his hip, then bent his throbbing organ downward until its sensitive tip made delightful contact with the wet, slippery fronds in her blossomed cleft. Slowly, tantalizingly, she slid it up and down the track.

"Like this?" And Aaron answered her, "Ummmm." She pulled it lower and thrust lightly with her hips, piercing herself with only the head. "And this?" To which Aaron advised her, "Ummmm." With her free hand she clutched one buttock and drew him toward her, accepting a quarter of his maleness inside her hot, pulsating passage. "Or this?" As another quarter entered, Aaron managed, "Ummmm—aaaaah!"

Aaron gulped and sucked in a long breath, then hunched his hips to drive another quarter of his raging manhood into her wetly welcoming nest. It became Rebecca's turn to make monotone replies as she impaled herself on the last three inches. "Yeeeeee!" and "Hhhhhhmmmmmmm."

Hilted, Aaron remained there for a long, thrilling time, watching in the dim starlight from outside the sparkle in Rebecca's eyes. It drove him to greater arousal to know how much she was enjoying it. Their surroundings dictated quiet, so he only gradually allowed his pelvis to rock back and forth in rhythm to the sway of the train car. Rebecca soon joined him to aid in optimum penetration. She wanted to howl in delight, and so did he. With great determination they struggled to suppress the healthy sounds of their wonder-making.

Little by little their rate increased. Faster and harder Aaron thrust into the tight channel that formed a heated furnace around his surging member. With consummate care they conserved their energies, held back their essence to enhance the exquisite sensation of their pairing. Faint at first, then with growing insistence, the hollow, dizzying sensation built in Aaron's belly. He was . . . almost . . . there. Any . . . second . . . now . . . he would—would . . . explo—

Vaguely Aaron felt the curtain brush over his head and shoulder. Then a sharp pain in his rump and left side banished the joyous titillation of his near-climax when he landed in the aisle of the Pullman car.

"Oh . . . my . . . Gaaawd," he groaned a lament.

Sleep-drugged heads popped out of several curtains and Aaron scrambled to cover himself. A pillow came flying out of Rebecca's bunk, then his longjohns. Through the roar of his embarrassment, Aaron thought for a moment that a hearty giggle accompanied the underwear. With the pillow for a screen, Aaron hastily covered the lower part of his nakedness and stood in the passageway. Flushing a furious scarlet, he tried to avoid any eye-contact with the other passengers as he summoned his dignity and climbed back into Rebecca's berth.

"I've . . . never been so em-embarrassed," he gulped in a whisper. "I just want to shrivel up and go away."

"S'okay so long as this doesn't," Rebecca teased, fingers seeking his penis. "Oh, fantastic, fabulous, it's not harmed a bit," she added a moment later, squeezing it.

"You mean . . . ? It's still . . . ?" Aaron blushed again. "I never gave *that* a thought. How could I have stayed . . . up th-through all that?"

"Don't question Fate, Aaron dearest. Get out of those fuzzy red things and let's try to get back where we were."

"If it takes a while," Aaron added, returning to a better mood. "I won't mind at all."

"Nor I. Only, hurry, beloved, I feel all . . . empty."

Soon they silently laughed his humbling and disconcerting experience into another wonderful coupling. This time, Rebecca took the precaution of putting up the safety net across the opening to the berth. In retrospect, it might have been more fulfilling if they had been able to

103

voice their ecstasy, but at the time neither cared a jot.

He had stolen one of the white-eyes' ponies, three to be exact, and ridden with all the speed he could out of the valley where the bad whites cut trees. Sweet Grass spent three days on the trail without finding any sign of his Shoshone people. All the while his mangled finger throbbed with pain and grew through red to a ghastly purple. At the old campsite, he rested himself, washed away dirt and the salt of his tears, and found a cache of corn and bean cakes made from grain traded away from the Navajo. That helped the ache in his belly. Then Sweet Grass began a slow walk in a widening spiral around the village limits. He led his remaining two horses and studied the ground.

Drag marks from a lodge bundle or travois gave him his first clue. Someone had neglected to wipe out such a telltale sign. Further on, he came upon an innocent-looking cluster of stones. The picture-words drawn in the damp earth beneath each quickly told him the location of the new camp. With no further need to waste time in tracking, Sweet Grass swung atop the smaller horse and drummed moccasined heels into its ribs.

At a quick canter he started off toward the refuge of his home village. During the journey a mountain thunderstorm came up. The terrible flash and crackle of lightning and thunder scared off one of the ponies and left him with but one. That one he rode on toward the Grandfather Star (Polaris) that never moved. Each night, like his father had taught him, he set his direction for the next day by its presence low on the northern horizon. Each morning he verified his course by sighting the White Bear Lady Star (Venus). By the morning after Rebecca and Aaron's unlikely encounter in the Pullman, only a narrow, cold stream with a waterfall and one moderate sized mountain separated him from his family.

Stripping off his only clothing, he tied breechcloth and

moccasins to the bridle of the pony with a length of limber willow branch. Only his waistband remained, from which hung the tiny medicine pouch that contained a sun-dried, shriveled piece of his umbilical cord. Sweet Grass took a gulp of air and entered the icy water astride his stolen horse.

On the other side, so eager had he become, he did not even pause to put on his clothes. Bare as the day he first breathed life he pounded heels into the slatted sides of the plodding animal he rode until it reached a shambling canter. Up and over the side and before his widening eyes he saw the lodges of his people, seeming to rise from the ground itself as he advanced.

Sweet Grass fairly shrieked at the village crier when he came within hearing range. "Go for Walks Around, go for Red Shirt. My friends have been murdered by white-eyes, White Rabbit is a prisoner!"

Black Hand, Sweet Grass's father, calmed the boy. The medicine man came and examined the ruined finger, amputated it to prevent gangrene, then cauterized the stump and put a salve dressing on it. His mother fussed over Sweet Grass and brought him a bowl of broth, then one of dog meat and vegetables.

"Cross-Eyes came to us," Black Hand told his son. "He told of Stone Boy being killed and you prisoner with White Rabbit. That is why we attacked them. Where were you?"

Sweet Grass blinked, arranging the events of his captivity while he stuffed chunks of stewed dog into his mouth. "At the place where the white-eyes cut the trees in long pieces. They had a little shed there."

Black Hand grunted. "We thought that to be the place the white-eyes go to do their private things, so we didn't burn it or look inside."

"The door would not open. They had a—a—a . . ."

"Lock," his father provided the unfamiliar English word.

"Yes, lock on it. We dug out at the back wall." Quickly

105

Sweet Grass described the events of his last night in the white men's camp, certain he would have to repeat it to the council.

". . . and I ran like White Rabbit said," Sweet Grass concluded to the intent faces of the council. "He never got free and I had to keep going, so I took three horses and started for our village."

Murmurs of approval went around the assembled men. Not so for Red Shirt. Angrily he stood to speak. "The white-eyes lose three horses and I've lost a son. We must go back and get him."

Angered by more harm done his people, Walks Around came to his feet and put an arm around Red Shirt's shoulder. "My son, we will ride again against the men responsible for these evil deeds."

"What if it had been my son who didn't get away, instead of your grandson, White Rabbit?" Black Hand asked, although certain of the answer.

Walks Around produced a fearsome scowl. "It would be the same. One boy dead, two more tortured by the white-eyes. We will not rest until we hunt every one of them down and kill them."

Chapter 11

He sat like a malignant spider at the center of his web, always occupying a table in a dimly lighted corner of each saloon they visited. Chris Starret asked the question. John Duffey did the looking around and brought likely subjects for Starret's scrutiny. So far, Flagstaff had not proven as fruitful as they had expected.

"We can't be too open about it around here," Starret had told his chief henchman. "Someone might remember our efforts later."

"What are we going to do, then? You wanted a hundred or so men, Chris."

Starret shifted his mood, lightened up. "Johnny my boy, I think the problem is there's too much work around Flagstaff. No one wants to take a chance of being shot as if he can earn his pay in a safer manner. We'll go to Prescott and Phoenix. Tucson, too, if we have to. Most of the fast guns, the ones for hire, hang out in the south, anyway."

"I like that. It'll take longer, but it will be worth it. I—ah—I've got one prospect over there at the bar."

"Send him over. Then you and the boys head for Prescott. You know what I'm looking for."

A gangling youth in his late teens, straw-yellow hair spiked with the dirt of neglect, ambled to the table. He touched the rim of his hat in a gesture of insolence and exposed crooked yellowed teeth. "Man says you got a job for me."

"*Sir*. Call me sir, or Mr. Starret, or get the hell out of my sight," Chris responded in a low, deadly tone.

Stiffening, the young drifter made his flat, watercolor blue eyes narrow. His shoulders hunched as he set himself to draw. An involuntary tic twitched the corner of his right eye.

"You wouldn't have a chance," Chris said in the same voice. "Tell me why I should consider hiring you."

Easing off, the human error licked his lips and forced a smile. "I take it that since you're looking for men in this way, whatever you're up to can't be legal. Being on the wrong side of the law's never bothered me."

Chris's cold stare fueled the kid's nervousness. "What else?"

Realizing he was about to be dismissed, the young man mulled over his possible responses. "I'm fast. And I hit what I aim at."

To the saddle tramp's surprise, Starret laughed. A long, low rumble increased to a clear sound of rueful amusement. "I like that. Looks like you might do. How do you feel about killing Indians? Any Indians?"

Swiftly the aspirant underwent a change. "Truth is, Mister Starret, Injuns just don't count. Killin' Injuns, Mezkins, and niggers don't build a man a reputation. I'm a feller lookin' for a reputation."

"Hummm. I see." Chris leaned forward, a peculiar light in his eyes. "Young man, I'm not talking about going out and shooting some blanket buck. You've heard of Colonel Chivington? I'm offering you an opportunity for all the killing, burning, looting, rape, and pillage your imagination could ever encompass. You'll wade knee-deep in blood, kill to your heart's content. And you'll be paid for it. Ten dollars a day while we are waiting to go, fifty a day when we're fighting."

A smile bloomed on the rat-faced youth. "Mister Starret, sir, I'd say you got yourself a man."

Other ears had heard the conversation meant for two. Chris Starret had noticed, though he gave no sign of it. A young soldier, not off duty, but in for a quick drink while on some detail from the small post at the edge of town, had been seated at the next table. He had nearly fallen sideways, craning to hear better. No sooner had the young would-be shootist made his final remark than the trooper had risen and hurried from the saloon. Allowing a few seconds to elapse, Chris Starret followed him.

Oblivious to any possibility of someone following him, the soldier headed straight to the blacksmith shop. A pump case had cracked at the post, backed into by a careless, inexperienced trooper's wagon. Neither the army's ferrier nor the wheelwright could weld cast iron, so he had been sent into town to have the repair made. While the blacksmith worked, he had indulged his longing for a cold beer. In the process he had heard something he felt sure Lieutenant Koenig would want to know. Perhaps even Lieutenant Colonel Alford. Increasing his pace, he turned into the alley that led to the back of the smithy.

Once off the main street, the noise diminished dramatically. It allowed the soldier to hear the rush of footsteps behind him. He started to turn when he felt the hot-cold violation of his body by the length of steel. He managed to twist his head enough to see and recognize the man who had been hiring gunslingers to kill Indians, a whole lot of Indians, from what he had overheard. It wouldn't matter now, he realized as the foreign object invaded his body again and sliced through his right kidney. Of its own accord, his body went rigid, rising on tiptoe, and he convulsed mightily as darkness slid across the blue sky and his wildly staring blue eyes began to cloud.

Chris Starret held on tightly unitl the life left his victim, then withdrew his Green River trade knife and wiped it on the blue shell jacket of the dead trooper. Slowly he lowered the body to the ground. Chris

109

resheathed his blade and started back toward the mouth of the alley. He whistled softly to himself, confident that now the word about the impending extermination of the Shoshone would not get around beforehand.

Solid jolts of the car shook Rebecca Caldwell out of her light doze. Mid-morning and already the powerful desert sun had heated the car enough that she had slipped off into light sleep. Beside her, Aaron Hawkins roused from his own post breakfast nap. He yawned and spoke through the distortion of it.

"What is it?"

Rebecca peered out the window. "I don't know. We're out in the middle of—of nowhere."

Aaron followed her gaze and cheered considerably. "Look out there to the north. It's what people are starting to call the Painted Desert. See all the colors?"

"It is . . . quite beautiful," Rebecca acknowledged. "Like a Navajo sand painting."

"Just so," Aaron said, beaming. "It also means we can't be far from Winslow." Far ahead, the locomotive chuffed and hissed in leashed immobility. It added an inviting background to his words. "Some folks are starting to get down. Why don't we go explore?"

On the sand and gravel of the desert, Aaron led the way forward. Nearing the stock car he heard the plaintive nicker of his horse. Concern for the animal's well-being wrinkled his brow. Then he saw the two flagmen. Each carried a square of red cloth on a stout staff. One headed past Aaron and Rebecca toward the rear of the train.

"I'll put down a new set of torpedoes," he called back.

"That explains it," Rebecca exclaimed.

"How? What?" Aaron blurted.

"I was dreaming. I thought I heard gunshots, but they didn't fit with the dream. It must have been the signal torpedoes."

"Ummm. Well, you know more about trains than I

110

do," Aaron prompted.

"When there's trouble on the track, work crews or other train crews put little packets of explosive on the tracks to warn any traffic behind them to slow and stop. They go off from compression. Let's go find out what's wrong," she urged.

Taking the lead, Rebecca strode forward, reaching the cowcatcher of the locomotive in time to hear the second flagman explain the situation to the engineer.

"Flash flood last night. Little Colorado went over its banks. Damned if it didn't wash out that trestle. It had been showing wear, but no one figured it for that. Didn't expect a storm like that, either."

"How long will it take the repair crew?" the engineer asked resignedly.

"Three, four days."

"That's impossible," the engineer thundered.

"Took out this end and the whole center span. We've got thirty men working."

"Then get more," the lord of the rails demanded.

Shrugging, the flagman answered mildly. "Any more would only get in each other's way. We have wagons to take the passengers in to the Barber Hotel in Winslow. Put 'em up at the railroad's expense. Best we can do, Hardy."

Rebecca and Aaron exchanged glances. "We can ride to Flagstaff from here in less time than that," the young lawman told her.

"Then let's do it. There's nothing we're interested in at Winslow."

It took considerable argument, and a jerry-rigged ramp to get the horses out before the train crew agreed to what they wanted. Rebecca also had to promise they would not put in for refunds on the unused portion of their tickets. At last, saddled and acclimated to solid ground again, Sila and Buck stood ready. Rebecca put all her skill at coquetry into her effusive thanks to the conductor and porters who had helped them. Then they set off on the

111

sixty-mile journey to Flagstaff.

Blackjack Duffey had extraordinary success in Prescott. A mine there had turned to a dry hole, and a lot of men found themselves unemployed. Few had any scruples about shooting Indians. He sent them on to the rendezvous site selected by Chris Starret. Their numbers grew steadily each day. By the time news of the trestle washout reached Flagstaff, fifty men had been added to the twenty-five Chris had assembled earlier. He felt the total sufficient for a little training operation he had in mind.

Scouts had located a small, mixed band of Shoshone and Ute, a hunting party, along the Little Colorado River near Gray Mountain. Following the noon meal, he sent his lieutenants to gather the men in the pools of shade under a trio of ancient oaks. When the grumbling and joshing died down, Chris stood before them and made his announcement.

"If you are anything like me, you're getting sick and tired of sitting here on your butts." Shouts of agreement answered him. "We've got a little clean-up job to do, keep you busy and take your minds off loafing among the trees."

"We ain't no rag-pickers," one hardcase protested.

"No. You're Indian fighters. At least that's what you told me. I propose to find out if that's true. There's some thirty redskins a day's ride northeast of here who need to be taught their manners. You all ready to go do that?"

A roar of agreement answered. "That's good. We spend the rest of today making ready, then ride out before dawn tomorrow. First off the scouts who found them have a few things to tell you. Then we'll decide how we're going to attack. After that every man tends to his own equipment. I want nothing that rattles or jingles. No shiny ornaments to flash in the sun and give us away. And every gun has to be clean, oiled, and in top shape.

Ammunition the same."

"Hey, you sound like the fuckin' army," a lanky gunhawk in his late twenties complained.

"That, friend, is why the army kicks the asses off Indians every time they attack the savages on their terms. You might as well have a baseball bat as a jammed rifle. Ammunition that won't discharge, or is too corroded to fit in the chambers, is sure to get a man killed in a big fight. We're not facing down Kansas plowboys with acne and itchy gunhands to build a reputation as bad guns. You'll work for your trophies, that I'll guarantee you. Now listen to Herb and Mick here."

Somewhat sobered by the two hours of briefing and planning, the men worked diligently on their equipment, weapons, and ammunition. Dry rations of jerky, pemmican, cornmeal, and dried apples were passed out. That night Chris noted a marked lack of drinking bouts and card games. As promised, the leaders among the huge gang roused them to coffee, hot biscuits, and fatback in time to depart an hour before sunrise.

After an all-day, circuitous course toward the Little Colorado River, they neared their unwitting quarry two hours before sundown. Chris maintained trail discipline, insisting on no smoking, and all cook fires to be made smokeless and put out before dark. "They're only two miles from here," he offered as reason enough.

Those who found easy sleep were awakened along with those who did not at two-thirty in the morning. Urged to take the greatest care, they worked their way into position over the next three hours. The silver-white bar of first light slashed across the east by the time the killers edged their way to three sides of the clearing. Orange glows from banked fires made animal eyes on the ground. Around them, pulled into their robes of bearskin or elk hide, the Shoshone and Ute slept. Chris Starret studied the situation while his satisfaction grew.

Slowly he drew his .45 Colt and cocked the hammer. He took careful aim at a slumbering figure and fired the

113

signal to attack. Howling like the tormented of hell, seventy men stormed out into the clearing, firing at the befuddled, shocked-awake Indians. To Chris's right a Ute screamed and clapped his hands to his face. Blood streamed between his fingers. Two hunters came to their knees and swiftly loosed arrows.

They had three each in the air before one fell to gunfire from the attacking hardcases. Two gunmen and a horse shrieked in pain from wounds inflicted by the courageous Indians. Everywhere the dark became light in the flash of yellow-orange muzzle bloom. Yelling a singular war cry, one Shoshone made a dash for his horse. In the general confusion he managed to get astride and lunged forward, wielding a lance with terrible accuracy.

Gutted by the steel lance point, the mouthy young gunman who had objected to the military requirements fell from his horse, both hands feebly trying to stuff his intestines back into the huge rent in his belly.

"He got Billy-Bob," a saddle tramp with a pronounced Southern accent blurted.

Chris took careful aim at the Shoshone with the lance. He squeezed off a round that sent a 250 grain load speeding toward the deadly menace. Hot lead punched through the brave's chest, three inches to the left of his heart. Though not before he buried his lance in the belly of another white marauder, who squealed like a pig and clutched at the shaft after the Shoshone let it go in reaction to being shot. Chris spent another bullet on the vengeful Indian and turned to seek new targets.

To both sides, Chris noticed that the firing had begun to dwindle. Pastel washes of pink, orange, and blue sent rayed bars across the east, and the scene began to resolve into clear visibility. Wherever he looked, Chris saw only the bodies of Indians on the ground. Not a one moved. His followers began to grin foolishly and dismount. They walked in among their vanquished foe and proceeded to strip the Indians of any item that took their fancy. Several of them, with an eye toward a profit, started for the horses.

"We did it," the scout, Mick, stated simply.

"Yep," Chris agreed, removing his hat to wipe his hairless crown. "Every damned one of them. I think the boys are ready for a real test now."

He had been born in the wild, mountainous country of Walnut Canyon. For his first year he had played and gamboled with his brothers and sisters. With the coming of what would correspond to a human's early teenage years, he had taken on solitary ways. He shunned his siblings and hunted alone. He sought a mate eventually, from another pride. Their five seasons together had been tumultuous at best.

His left ear had been ravaged in one lustful mating encounter. In his turn he had swatted his mate in the nose with an open-clawed paw and left permanent scars. By the chronological age of twelve he had left behind all vestiges of cougar family life. A rock slide had broken his hip during that year and he nearly starved. He healed with a permanent disfigurement that caused him to limp and to be slow. Somehow his appetite had failed to adjust to this affliction.

Always hungry, he sought easier prey. By the spring of his thirteenth year, he built up courage enough to drift close in to human habitations. He eyed the docile animals left out to graze: their young when they came proved particularly vulnerable. For two years he lived in a welter of plenty. Then the two-legged ones had surprised him with a fresh kill. The barbed shafts they shot into his side and left leg hurt terribly. They also served to reduce his agility by even more. In desperation, then, he had taken the last irrevocable step.

He took down a young one of the two-legged—a stray which had wandered into the forest of the canyon and become lost. It made small, bleating sounds like the white, fluffy four-legs the two-legs kept. Sensing his opportunity, his stomach cramped with hunger, he pounced.

How sweet, how tender. Such succulent meat. Having acquired a taste for human flesh, the heady aroma of human blood, the aging, crippled cougar changed his behavior once again. Now he hunted only man.

He slid through the screen of tall, dark green firs and juniper, stalking two such beings. They sat atop two of the four-legged whose young he had found so tasty—before he learned how much better the two-legged tasted. They made sounds back and forth, much like he had done with his litter mates when they were small, cuddly cubs. Did they, too, communicate the pleasures of their day?

"I'm glad we camped by that waterfall, Aaron. I was ready to kill for a bath. And you were so tender, so helpful and adoring. You didn't really have to scrub my back."

"I wanted to. Besides, it got us warmed up for some powerful loving."

"Beast. Is that all you think about?" Rebecca said in mock disapproval.

"It didn't used to be. But that was before I met you."

"Oh, pooh. Tonight. You wait and see. Where *do* we camp tonight?"

"I'm not sure. I've not been up this way before. Finding the waterfall was sheer luck," he admitted.

"Aaron . . . you're so precious." Rebecca burbled. *Get ahold of yourself, sister*, she chided. *You sound like a silly schoolgirl.*

Aaron made an expression of puzzled astonishment. "I've been called a lot of things, but never that. What did you have in mind for tonight?"

Their voices faded as the cougar dropped back. He could stalk them no longer. Besides, they were full grown, and the two of them could represent danger. They had led him to a familiar place, though. They rode into the valley where the tender ones lived. He would wait, and watch, and food would come to him.

116

Chapter 12

Rays of sunlight broke around a small, black-bellied
charcoal cloud and shimmered with iridescent splendor
off the wings of a multi-colored flock of pigeons. The
gentle, curious birds flew in disorganized formation
around the largest edifice in the wide, flat valley. The
two-story native granite structure, with a tall central
tower, dominated the landscape. Built of the same
material, four large, warehouses formed a wide square
around it. Scattered here and there among the other
structures, Rebecca Caldwell identified half a dozen
small, single-story houses built of log and stone. The
remaining dozen or so had a less permanent appearance.
Farther out, several log cabins with sod roofs sat among
neatly tilled fields.

There was a grainery, its elevator not quite so tall as
the stone tower, an open, airy place roofed in split logs
that must be a blacksmithy, a rock milk house by the
stream, and a large pig sty, with an octagonal smokehouse
close at hand for the products of the big, muddy pen.
Riding down out of the pass to Walnut Canyon, Rebecca
and Aaron soon heard the tinkle of tiny bells. They grew
in number and size until a huge bass tocsin in the tower
began to peal mournfully. Their approach scattered a
large flock of sheep tended by barefoot and bare-legged
boys of ten and twelve. By the time they reached the

village square, a sizable number of people had gathered.

"What have we here?" Rebecca asked from the side of her mouth.

"I'm not sure," Aaron responded in kind. "I've never heard of anything like this."

All of the women, Rebecca noted, wore baggy, ankle-length unadorned, dull brown pullover dresses that came barely short of being habits. Children of both genders were clothed in plain garments of gray, lightweight cloth that slipped on over the head. The men, likewise uniformly dressed, had their hair bowl-cut, with shaved pates that gave them a monk's tonsure. They also wore what appeared to be the basic good quality *chlamys* of Ancient Rome, the tunic hems even cut in square scallops and embroidered in bright colors. Most had needlework adornment on the yoke, around the rectangular neckhole. While the women went barefoot, the men had sturdy sandals with heel pieces and high laces. One man stood apart, apparently the leader, distinguished by the purple-edged toga he wore over his tunic. Although not unlike the similarity of dress in an Indian village, these costumes gave Rebecca a hint of distinct uneasiness.

"Welcome travelers to the Congregation of Heavenly Pilgrims. I am Father Asmodeus," the overdressed leader intoned in a rumbling baritone.

"I am Aaron Hawkins," Aaron responded, his own sense of strangeness prompting him to omit being the deputy U. S. marshal for the area. "And this is Rebecca Caldwell. We are on our way to Flagstaff."

Asmodeus frowned deeply. "A place of sin and suffering. It is filled with unbelievers, and those who worship gold instead of the True One. You would be well advised not to go there."

"Unfortunately, I must," Aaron countered. "I—ah—have business there."

Again the scowl. Asmodeus glanced from Aaron to Rebecca, her clear loveliness and obvious youth. "Dark business, I suppose."

Aaron wanted no more of this moralistic fencing. "That depends upon how you look at the law and justice."

"Laws are a thing of man and unclean in the eyes of the True One," Asmodeus condemned.

Her own temper pricked, Rebecca made bold to prod him. "But aren't most laws based upon the Commandments of God? Not to kill, not to steal, to keep the Sabbath holy?"

Now the scowl became a thunderous expression of outrage. "This woman has a tongue with sharp edges," he said in a warning tone. "She should learn her proper place, and the virtue of silence."

Instantly Rebecca had a hot reply ready to give. Before she uttered it, a tall, strapping example of ideal Nordic manhood stepped forward, his broad shoulders cutting a swath through the throng. His clear, Norwegian sky eyes twinkled with amused intelligence. Crossing thigh-thick forearms over his chest, he valiantly challenged the patriarch.

"These travelers are not of our Holy Pilgrimage, Father Asmodeus," he declared in a heavy Scandinavian accent. "Their ways are not ours, *ja* sure. Although now subject to your will, they have not yet learned what you command."

"We are in the process of enlightening them, Hagar," Asmodeus responded in a chilly tone that bore frightful warning. Several women covered their faces with a tail of their headscarves and looked away.

"The young man is right," Rebecca took up. "We would, of course, abide by your rules while among you. But we need to know what they are before we can be held accountable."

"This woman continues to defy the True One's commandments," Asmodeus snapped, ignoring Rebecca further and turning to Aaron. "And what is your business with the law? Are you one of Satan's princes;

a lawyer?"

Aaron sighed and revealed his badge. "I am the deputy U. S. marshal for this territory. I am charged, as it seems you are, with enforcing the law."

"Man's law—a puny reed in the face of the justice of the True One."

"No doubt, Asmodeus," Aaron agreed. "Though we are in need of food and shelter for the night. Then we will be gone from your valley and trouble you no more."

Father Asmodeus changed, became the genial host. "You are welcome to both. Hagar, find a place for them both with our band of pilgrims," he instructed, placing them in the charge of the blond giant.

Rebecca and Aaron dismounted, and Hagar led them a short distance, then paused. For the first time he took in the visitors. His worshipful expression and the hot glow in his big, blue eyes advertised his opinion of Rebecca Caldwell.

"I am Hagar Olaf. I am new to the Congregation of Heavenly Pilgrims. And I have enough of the manners of outsiders left to heartily welcome you to our valley, *ja* sure."

"Thank you, Hagar, that's very kind," Rebecca said sincerely. Hagar all but wriggled like a petted puppy.

"Father Asmodeus is rather strict about things around here," Aaron observed.

"It must be that way to keep the Congregation together and free from sin," Hagar recounted as though quoting a memorized bit of dogma.

"Yes," Aaron went on, treading dangerous ground. "Do you know anything about the origin of his name?"

"No. I never thought to ask, pie-golly," Hagar admitted, his broad Scandinavian features blank.

"Asmodeus, along with Beel—." Rebecca silenced him with a hard, cautionary scowl. "Ah—yeah—he-he, we'll save that for another time. Where do we stay?"

"We can put Miss Rebecca with Sister Caroline, and you can stay with me."

He had remembered her name. Another tingle of unease rustled along Rebecca's spine. Yet she had so far not encountered anything specific or material to show for cause. She followed Hagar to one of the stone-and-log dwellings, somewhat larger than most. A gaggle of towheaded children, indeterminate of sex in identical straight-hem tunics and soup-bowl haircuts, with bare legs and feet, swarmed around one corner of the house, yelling merrily.

They effusively greeted the visitors, and the eldest called for their mother. She came in a moment, a plain, almost drab women in her mid-thirties, with her hair done in a long, gathered hank that hung down her back. Badly worn by chores, climate and bearing seven children in ten years, she already had the deeply graven lines of a woman twenty years her elder on her face.

"How may I serve you?" she asked in a quiet voice, not looking directly into the face of either male.

"These are visitors, Sister Caroline. They are in need of lodging. The woman will stay with you."

"Yes, Brother Hagar," Sister Caroline answered dully.

"When you next hear the bell ring, it is the time for ablutions," Hagar instructed Rebecca and Aaron. "When next it tolls, we will gather for the evening meal in the Great Hall on the north side of Temple Square."

"You take your meals together?" Rebecca asked, surprised.

"Kitchens waste space in our houses. The True One hates waste," Caroline answered.

After Hagar departed with Aaron, Caroline had little to say. "These are my children. Josiah, he's ten; Jezreel, she's nine; Jeremiah, seven; Japheth, six; Jedidah, five; her twin sister, Jerusha; and little Jimna. He's three. You'll sleep in the girls' loft. Take off those mannish boots so you look the proper woman. We sing as we march to our meals. I hope you have a good voice."

With that she left Rebecca among the children. Two of the girls tugged at her hands. "We'll show you where you'll sleep."

"You really must get rid of those awful boots," Jezreel said primly. "Only men are permitted to have footwear. And you can borrow one of my head scarves. Only men . . ."

"I know, are permitted to wear hats," Rebecca concluded sharply, her discontent growing.

"Are those real?" Josiah asked, indicating Rebecca's brace of Colt Bisleys. "I've never seen a woman with a gun before."

"I've never seen a gun before," Jeremiah added wistfully.

She might have seen them for the first time, the way Jezreel reacted to the pair of .45-Colt revolvers. "Oh, my!" she squeaked. "You absolutely mustn't have those. Firearms are forbidden, even to the men."

Rebecca gave her a hard look. "I'm sorry, but there is where I draw the line. I will not put away my guns, except to go into a church."

Jezreel gave her a blank, stricken look. "You can't go into the Temple, you aren't one of us. And I don't mean to put them up, you must destroy them at once. Guns are evil."

That proved a bit more than Rebecca could handle tactfully. "Guns aren't evil, they're inanimate objects. Only living beings have the capacity for good or evil."

"Firearms are the tools of Satan," Caroline reappeared suddenly to say ringingly in support of her daughter's argument. "They lay in wait to entice people to sin."

"That's insane," Rebecca blurted. "Only human beings have a brain that can formulate intent. My revolvers are no different in that light than—than that rock there. Can it *will* itself to do harm?"

"They are not the same. Father Asmodeus says so. It's in the Book of Hours. To bring them here is to invite all manner of calamity to enter our valley. That's why you must demolish them immediately," Caroline demanded, her face hot, eyes alight with righteous indignation.

Rebecca had long ago learned the futility of arguing with the self-righteous, fanatics and the smugly pseudo-superior. Her last forbearance cracked. "Like hell I will. I'd rather sleep under a tree than be subjected to such blind ignorance and mindless prejudice. We can always ride on, you know."

Profound change came over Caroline. Her flushed face drained, and a tremble came to her lower lip. "Oh, no, no. Perhaps I spoke too hastily. You are strangers and not bounden by our holy ordinances. I only sought . . . to enlighten."

Such flawed enlightenment the world can well do without, Rebecca thought, but she chose other words. "Forgive my temper. I have lived in the midst of violence most of my life," Rebecca informed the mother of seven. "Without the aid and protection of a gun, I'd be hardly more than a slave today. We see the same thing differently, but I know for certain that guns are no more good than they're evil. They simply *are*. It is up to those who use them as to the result. Now, please, can't we be friendly toward each other? At least for the short time Aaron and I will be here."

"You aren't leaving soon, are you?" Caroline asked, almost pleadingly.

Why the sudden change? Rebecca could think of nothing said or done to justify it. "Tomorrow morning. We must get on to Flagstaff, as I said before."

Caroline turned away, her brow gullied with a troubled frown. Rebecca found herself confronted by a wide-eyed Josiah. Beside him stood Jeremiah. With a wistful sigh, Josiah reached out unexpectedly and stroked the curved backstrap of Rebecca's left-hand Bisley with nail-bitten fingers.

"You're wonderful," he spoke softly. "And—and I don't hate guns."

"Someone around here has a little sense," Rebecca muttered to herself as she turned away to follow Jezreel into the house.

Even with the information given to them by the Indian boys, scouts from Chris Starret's private army had to do extensive searches to discover the new location of Walks Around's village. Notwithstanding their losses in the "training maneuver," as Chris had styled the attack on Ute and Shoshone hunters, the eighty-four-man force rode easy in the saddle along the clearly marked course. Seven abreast, they made an impressive formation.

Twelve ranks deep, horses churned the sod into a loamy, red-brown mire. Slightly ahead of the body of self-styled Indian fighters, Chris Starret and John Duffey led the way through the rolling terrain of the Kaibab Plateau. Although he said nothing about it, Chris could not lose his unease, knowing that the Navajo reservation lay only a couple of hours' travel to the east.

In the past, the Navajo had been considered fierce warriors, conquerers of nearly two-thirds of Arizona and northern New Mexico. They could be again. Would they fight to aid an old enemy, the Shoshone?

"Damn clever," he said aloud.

"What is?" John Duffey inquired.

"Not what, who. The Shoshone chief was sure clever in where he picked his new campsite. We've got the Ute on our left and the Navajo on the right," Chris elaborated. "If either got the idea to help out the Shoshone against us, we'd never live to tell about it."

"Hell, those Injuns fight amongst each other more than they do against the white man," Duffey depreciated. "This is prime hunting country, and all three tribes claim it. If anything, it'll work to our advantage."

Chris hazarded a relieved smile. "That's why I have you around, Blackjack. You're just chock-full of good advice. According to Buhler and the other scout who found 'em, we've got another half an hour before we dismount this herd of scalawags. That leaves a mile approach on foot, a night's rest, and half a mile more to be in position."

"Kellogg's layin' out a lot of money for this crew," Duffey observed.

"Yeah. It comes off the top, so that means your cut and mine are less. We've got to make this one count."

Every morning of his life for as long as he could remember, Walks Around rose early to greet the Sky Father. At least he had, with the exception of those times when there had been dancing all night to celebrate a great victory over some enemy, like the Arapaho, or a good hunt. Although his ancient bones ached, he would not deviate from this devotion to the Spirits this crisp, cool dawn. Grunting softly, he turned back the sleeping robes and sat up to put on moccasins. Then he rose and slipped into his breechcloth and a hunting shirt.

This addition of clothing had come recently. As a boy he had greeted the Sky Father naked. In the seasons after his dreaming time, and all those after, he had worn only a loin covering and moccasins. Advanced years dictated a bit more protection from the high-altitude chill. On this day, unaccountably, he took along his favorite bow and a quiver of arrows. War shafts, not the thicker hunting projectiles.

"Waugh! What a terrible taste in my mouth," Walks Around murmured as he stirred himself and stepped over the sleeping forms of his two younger sons, still without mates and living at home.

It did his heart good to recall that he had seen more than four two-hands of seasons when he got the youngest, Fat Beaver, on his wife, Sweet Wind. Now a stripling of fourteen seasons, he still had the darling features of his mother. A knife stab of old grief touched Walks Around's heart, remembering Sweet Wind. She

125

had given up her life to provide him with another son. He would remember to mention her secret name to the Sky Father in his greeting.

Outside the lodge, Walks Around guided himself by the soft orange glow of banked cook fires. Here and there he saw an industrious woman up early to kindle new flames with small twigs. Their men should be well pleased. They would have full, warm bellies to begin the day with. Walks Around padded on through the relocated village. Not far to the east lay a sharp drop-off, a cliff, actually. There he could be alone and talk with the lord of the day.

Reaching his chosen spot, he lay aside his bow and quiver and turned to the graying blackness where the Sky Father would rise again as he had each morning of the people's history. Walks Around raised his arms in preparation and took a deep breath. The first stanza of the welcoming song had to be sung without interruption. There it came, the pale gray line, low on the distant hills. Intense white followed, blurred along the bottom with pastel pink.

Walks Around breathed deeply again and opened wide to start the chant. A moment before he could sing the words, the first crack of an enemy's rifle shattered the calm of dawn.

They came in a rush, a wide sweep down a shallow decline toward the western end of the village. Not until the bloodlusting private army reached the first lodges did they make a sound. At Starret's command, they held fire and waited for clear, easy targets. The first to fall were two old women. One dropped face first into her cook fire. The other died trying to reach the entrance to her lodge. Chris swung his arm in a wide arc, indicating that the charging men swing right and left to rake the whole community with gunfire.

A fusillade opened up, punching bullets through the

126

flimsy walls of brush summer lodges and hide tepees. Dogs set up a yapping, horses neighed and swung one way and another in the herd. Then arrows filled the air. At several spots Shoshone men opened up with rifles.

"Get the torches going," Chris ordered. "Burn these damned lodges. You, Guthery, take your picked men and cut out the ponies. Over there, Burns, ride for that knot of warriors. Break 'em up before they start hitting some of us."

Beside him, John Duffey methodically took aim and fired at scurrying women and children. Easy targets, and far less dangerous than taking on warriors. He sighted in on a lad in his early teens who had bolted from the largest lodge, a bow and quiver in hand. The bullet kicked up dust behind Fat Beaver's heels, and the lad sprinted for the dubious cover of a fallen tree trunk that formed one side of the ring around the central fire pit. From there he loosed an arrow that pierced the right side of one white man's chest.

"Get that kid," Duffey shouted as the momentum of the attack carried him past the spot.

Startled by the sudden, unexpected attack, Walks Around snatched up his bow and quiver and began to run through the village. He called out to several select men, including his son, Red Shirt, and gave the rallying cry. At the center of the village he found his youngest son crouched behind the log used as a back rest by the council members at public gatherings. Blood ran in a thin sheet from a shallow surface scrape an enemy bullet had caused. In the fleeting second he looked at his boy, Fat Beaver released another arrow.

Running straight, the shaft hummed through the air and embedded itself in the left eyesocket of a hardcase from Starret's original gang. In the moments of life he had left, the outlaw pawed ineffectually at the dangling projectile, then uttered a soulful groan and fell from

127

his saddle.

"You shoot well, my son," Walks Around complimented him.

Fat Beaver gave his father a jaunty wave and notched another arrow. By now the main force had swarmed through the village, and were behind father and son. Walks Around saw two storehouses aflame, and counted some ten lodges burning. The rattle of gunfire behind him reminded him of the danger. He and Fat Beaver turned in time to see the whites make their second charge through the village.

Chapter 13

"Damn, there's more of them than I thought," John Duffey observed when he reached Chris Starret's side.

"Must be gathering warriors from other bands to . . . do something. All the better we hurt them now."

"We're takin' big losses, Chris. I'm not so sure we outnumber them at all. Worse, we don't have surprise to work for us any more."

"You've got a point. We'll take another run through the village, fire anything that isn't burning, and kill all we can. Then we head out."

Relieved, Duffey nodded assent. He spurred off to relay the new tactics. Within two minutes, Chris signaled for the next charge. Hooting and howling, the vengeful whites thundered down to the embattled village. Three young women, driven from their lodges by fire, ran blindly into the line of attack. Chortling lustfully, a trio of white invaders scooped them off their feet and rode away in the predetermined line of withdrawal. They'd have time for a little fun later on, they reasoned. Near the center of the camp, John Duffey pointed to Fat Beaver.

"There, get that kid. He's entirely too good with a bow."

Before he could act on his own suggestion, an arrow, fired by Fat Beaver, smacked into the broad, churning chest of his horse. The wounded beast uttered a nearly human squeal and went stiff legged. The hard jolt from the animal's forehoofs and his instant collapse sent John Duffey sprawling. He rolled twice and came to his knees. As he gained his feet and raised an arm, Chris Starret swung close by his side and they hooked elbows.

Duffey swung up and onto the saddle skirt behind Chris and they loped off to the south, following the prescribed route. Around them the final shots were being fired, while the attackers sought to break off and withdraw. Already Duffey could hear the wailing lamentations of the Indian women. It faded quickly as they galloped away.

Aaron Hawkins awoke two hours before sunrise. He dressed quietly and completed his packing, habit and taste buds crying out for coffee. He would have to forego it, Aaron realized, if they wanted to get successfully away. Convinced that something decidedly unnatural and unpleasant had a grip on this religious community he suspected they might have difficulty leaving if they waited until the Heavenly Pilgrims had all awakened. He walked to the small stone house where Rebecca had spent the night. There he paused at the door a moment, conflicting emotions tugging within him.

His knock went unanswered. Aaron rapped again, louder. He heard a faint scurrying and then the snick of a night bolt being thrown. The door swung open a crack and he saw a small, clear blue eye peering out. There was a gasp and the portal swung wide.

"Oh, it's you," tumbled out of Josiah. The ten-year-old stood there without a stitch on.

"I've come for Miss Rebecca. We have to leave," Aaron explained, ignoring the lad's embarrassment over his nakedness.

"Sure. I understand. C'mon in. I'll—ah—get dressed and let her know you're here. But be quiet. My maw would kill us all."

For a moment, Aaron believed the boy meant it literally. Josiah scuttled off in the dark. Then his bare back flashed white in a shaft of moonlight as he climbed a ladder to a loft sleeping room. He returned in a moment, in his basic shiftlike garment, and crossed in front of the cold fireplace and up another ladder. Before Aaron could count to five, the youngster appeared again and spoke in a harsh whisper.

"She's almost ready."

Brightness flared and turned to the steady yellow of a kerosene lamp. "What's the meaning of this?" Caroline demanded.

"We're leaving," Aaron told her curtly.

"But you can't," Caroline nearly wailed. "It's not possible. Far too dangerous," she babbled on. "Josiah, go for Father Asmodeus. These folks can't be permitted to leave."

"I'll not go," the little lad said stubbornly. "They ain't part of us and it ain't their problem."

"What problem?" Rebecca asked from the loft above.

"It's—it's the demon beast," Caroline said faintly. "It will stalk you and kill you."

"A . . . demon? Come now, Caroline, you're good, godly folks. Surely you can't believe in demon animals! Creatures possessed? That sort of thing went away with the Middle Ages," Rebecca gently chided.

"But we can't let you go," Caroline gasped in desperation.

"Why not? Frankly I can't understand this at all. Yesterday evening you made such a fuss over my sixguns, my clothes, everything. I'd think you'd be glad to be done with us once and for all."

"I would," Caroline hastened to declare. "We all would. You're . . . contaminated by the world outside. And yet . . ."

"Tell me about this demon beast."

131

"I can't. I dare not. We have an obligation to protect all life. Even the unsaved and unwashed. You cannot go out there."

"Nevertheless, we shall," Rebecca assured her. She dropped her saddlebags and a large carpetbag to the floor and started down the ladder.

"Josiah, do as you're told. Run for Father Asmodeus."

Lower lip out in a pink pout, arms crossed over his shallow chest, the little boy remained steadfast. When Rebecca reached the ground floor, he stepped forward and hefted the carpetbag.

"I'll help you at the corral," he announced. Then, with a backward look over one shoulder, "Then I'll go for Father Asmodeus."

With Josiah's agile assistance it took only three minutes to cut out Šila and Buck. Quickly and wordlessly, Rebecca and Aaron saddled their mounts. The packhorse had its X-frame pack saddle cinched into place and loaded. When they at last made ready to step into stirrups, Josiah spoke softly, a winsome, pleading tone in his voice.

"I wish I could go with you." Bare toe scuffing the dirt, he looked eagerly from one to the other, then at the ground. "Yeah, I know. What would you do with a kid on your hands? I *hate* it here. I hate these dumb clothes. Most of all I hate Father Asmodeus. His rules say us kids can't run and play, laugh or whistle. We have to 'toil in the vineyard,' and keep a—ah—'serious demeanor,' suited to the 'Coming of the Lord.'" Josiah struck a pose, legs apart, fists on hips, scrawny elbows akimbo. He canted his head to one side. "Boy, to hear him tell it, you'd think that was going to be any minute now. We ain't got a vineyard, but we do a whole lot of toiling."

Touched by the little boy's appeal, Rebecca would have willingly agreed to take him along to a place where he could be a normal boy. Yet the entire situation at the religious center made her so uneasy she abolished such

132

thoughts. Instead she reached out and patted his fine, snow-white hair, then clasped a warm, soft palm to each cheek. She tilted Josiah's face up toward hers.

"Don't ever lose that spirit of rebellion. Whenever you encounter something your reason and heart tell you is wrong, don't be afraid to stand up against it. If it were at all possible, I'd gladly take you along. As it is, we're going the wrong way, toward the wilderness and danger. Besides, there's this 'demon beast.' Trying to make sure you were safe could cost all of us our lives."

Josiah caught a note of skepticism in Rebecca's remark about the deadly, unknown menace. Face twisted with anguish, he spoke with stirring conviction. "Oh, it's real enough. I saw it once. It—it kills people."

"Then you're better off here, Josiah. Take care of your brothers and sisters and try to find another way to resist Father Asmodeus's teachings. Good-bye, now."

Lunging forward impulsively, Josiah wrapped his arms around Rebecca's waist. "I love you, Miss Rebecca."

Detaching herself from the boy, Rebecca mounted and rode out with Aaron. Bound by his grudging obedience to his mother, Josiah trotted off to the big house on Temple Square where Father Asmodeus lived to inform him of their guests' leaving.

Asmodeus's reaction frightened the boy in its violence. The religious leader hurled a chair across the room, cursed with words Josiah had never before heard, and cast about the room like a caged animal.

"We can't allow it. They are our only hope. Somehow, someone has to bring them back. Josiah, go and fetch Elder Perkins, Deacon Banner, and Brother Tobias. Also Brother Hagar."

When Josiah had awakened and summoned the designated Pilgrims, he returned with them to the big house, and its three wives and eleven children. Quiet as a mouse, Josiah stood in a corner and listened to Father Asmodeus's instructions.

133

"Go after them. Bring them back. Offer whatever you must, promise anything, but bring them back. We have to have their help or we all perish."

"Hey, Chris, let's rein up an' take care of these sweet li'l gals," Jude Cross shouted above the rumble of hoofs.

"We haven't got time," Chris declined.

"Aw, come on, Chris. My pecker's stiff as a board, thinkin' about humpin' one of them," Randy Burke pleaded.

Angered by this minor rebellion, Chris signaled for a halt. Billows of dust engulfed the outlaw band as they reined their horses and milled about. Encouraged, Randy Burke swung from his saddle and yanked his captive off, throwing her roughly onto the ground.

"Spread your legs, gal, you're gonna get a thrill," he grunted while he groped at his fly.

"No, she's not. You horny sons-of-bitches made a big mistake. If we'd left those women behind, we wouldn't have to worry about pursuit. As it is, we've got to figure the Shoshone are hot after us," Chris declaimed. "Now, I want you to turn those women loose so we can make better time."

"We gonna poke them first?" Jude Cross asked expectantly.

"Hell no," John Duffey growled. "Not unless you want to stay behind and lose your hair."

"God damn it, we got a right to some pokey-pokey," one of the new men complained. "We took a lot of risk, tore up that Injun village, and got away with a few cuts and scrapes to remember it by. Now we have a go at the spoils of battle."

"I said no," Chris announced in a tone that engendered unease in those who knew him well. "Leave them and let's get on our way."

"I'm gonna get a little from all three first," the

rebellious gunhand persisted.

"Climb on your horse and get to moving," Chris menaced.

"Or what?"

"Or I'll kill you."

Chris's threat hung in the air, baited and deadly. A variety of emotions played across the obstinate gunhawk's face. His eyes narrowed, and he slid his hand to the butt-stock of his .45 Colt Peacemaker. With a small grunt of nervous energy, he grasped the black hard rubber grips and yanked his iron.

Chris Starret drew and shot him in the shoulder before the seven-inch barrel cleared leather. "What I said goes for everyone. Turn those Indian women loose and we ride. Now."

In the low light of a flickering fire, ten agile, lean, young men—boys in their mid to late teens, actually—stood before the stern-faced chief and five of the council. Outside the lodge, the sounds of mourning continued unabated, except for sleep, since the white men attacked the village. Walks Around looked at the supple limbs of the youthful messengers and wondered again how a mere passage of a few seasons could have so stealthfully robbed him of the same springy vitality.

Once he would have contested heatedly with other village boys for the honor of going on such a mission. Now his old bones rebelled at what he knew must be done, now and later on. Although evidence clearly indicated his rivals on the council had been right, Walks Around held to his earlier convictions. He wanted blood, to avenge the people, the band and tribe. But he wanted only the blood of those guilty. To that end, he carefully worded his instructions to the swift messengers about to be sent out to neighboring bands of Shoshone and to the Utes, Piutes, and Navajo.

"Tell them this: Walks Around, he of many coups and scalp locks, once more takes up the war pipe. He calls on all brave men to follow him. This is a war against a special enemy. He is a white enemy. But not all whites are the enemy. The digger-planter whites are to be left alone. Those whites who build their lodges into villages and stay within the village land are not to die. Those whites who scrape the ground for the yellow metal, if they make signs of peace, are not to die. Only the men who cut trees, and the soldiers who wear no man's uniform and fight for the tree killers, these are to die."

Walks Around paused and bent to a pile of beaded strips of deerskin, soft and pliable, worked in white, with red splotches, like drops of blood. He slung them on his left arm and began to pass them out. "Fire Carrier, take these two to the Utes, to their leaders, Cahdo and Umchak, from whom we have passage to our hunting grounds. Ask that they send warriors. Big Nose, you go among the Navajo, seek their most powerful singer, and have him call the young men to war." On it went until all the belts had been distributed. "Say that they are to gather here when the Sun Father rises seven times from today. Then we will strike at the heart of this white evil."

Red-winged blackbirds preened their glossy feathers on the limbs of stately pines. The sun felt warm on Rebecca Caldwell's back as she and Aaron Hawkins rode along the poorly defined trail that wound through the forested slopes of the northern range of the Mazatzal Mountains. Given a better road, which Aaron promised further on, they would make Flagstaff about mid-morning the next day. Dappled by shadows from overhead branches as the sun rose, Rebecca found their excursion utterly peaceful. When they stopped to give their mounts a blow, she spoke from her recent reflections.

"Did you notice the rather intense attention that big,

136

strapping blond fellow paid me? Hagar, the one you stayed with."

"Yes," Aaron grunted, at once jolted from his pacific mood. "I saw him. And I have to admit I was beginning to worry a bit. If he's built like that all over, he could put a bull elk to shame."

Light, tinkling laughter came from deep in Rebecca's throat. "Why, Aaron, you have no need to feel deprived. Nevertheless, I'm delighted. It's good for a man to be a bit jealous. It certainly flatters me. Better still, it perks up my outlook after the last thirty-six hours."

"You—ah—felt it too?" Aaron prodded.

"Oh, yes. I'm sure something is bothering those Heavenly Pilgrims. The women went on and on about the 'demon beast,' and even our little apostate Josiah warned us about it. That's one thing, but there seems to be an even more ominous situation that none of them will say anything about."

"Perhaps," Aaron suggested lightly, unconvinced, "they have some dark secret to hide? Maybe they sacrifice newborn infants to some forbidding god of blood and thunder. Or they might perform the Black Mass," he teased.

"*Aaron!* I'm serious. There's . . . something not quite right about that whole setup. Let's mount up. We've got a lot more miles to cover."

Luther Trask peered through over-long, greasy yellow bangs at the eight raggedly dressed youths who sat on rocks around him. His billowing, aged, oft-mended white linen duster—now graying to black, owing to a long absence from any laundry—flapped about his shins, which added to the scarecrow appearance of his long, lank, scrawny frame. He wore an odd arrangement of firearms, three in number.

Two .44 Remington Model '60 Army revolvers, still with the original percussion cap cylinders, nestled in holsters slung low on his legs, from separate tooled-leather belts. Slanted across his belly was a sewn leather tube affixed to a third belt. It contained a contrastingly new, nickle-plated Smith & Wesson .44 Frontier DA with pearl handles. The six-inch barrel had been cut down to three-and-a-half and recrowned. It made a fast, nasty belly gun with which Kid Trask, as he styled himself, was rumored to have murdered three men; one a fat, unarmed drummer who traveled in silver candlesticks and tea sets. The seventeen-year-old Kid Trask was said to have gone into a rage when he tried to sell the contents of the salesman's display case and learned that it was silver plate, not solid silver as advertised, and a thin plating job at that. Now he affected his fiercest sneer and addressed the complaints of his companions.

"I don't give a shit what Chris Starret said. Who's he, anyway? Had no right to turn us down. Me, especially. I've killed my men and I can handle a gun good as anybody."

"Nobody said you couldn't, Kid," Jake Ramsey hastened to assure his best friend and the nominal boss of their small outlaw band. "It's just . . . well, Starret's got him a rep. Wouldn't have done to buck him too hard."

"Where d'you hear he had a reputation?" Kid Trask challenged.

"Over New Mexico way, when I still lived with my folks. He an' six others kicked the shit outta a gang of forty Mex banditos down Chihuahua way, in the mountains," Jake persisted, looking up at his hero shyly through long lashes.

"Bull. A baldheaded old man like that?" the Kid dismissed.

"He ain't old. You see how smooth his skin is. Burned brown as an Injun, but young-lookin'," Arlow Cutter contradicted.

"Smooth, huh? Well, maybe he's a pantywaist, a sissy-boy," Kid Trask snarled.

Jake flushed a soft pink. The Kid's words hurt him. For

the past three years, since Jake's abandoned mother had moved into Arizona Territory, he and Luther had had a close, warm friendship. Often he and the Kid had . . . done things, which the Kid's harsh words denied and put to shame. Confused, and sensitive for a lad barely sixteen, Jake didn't know what to say.

"Whatever that old fart used to be, he's not bossin' us now. We came here to make a reputation for ourselves. Once we get rollin', doing business for ourselves, Starret will beg us to join up. If we're bad enough, even the Daltons will want us to throw in with 'em."

Arlow Cutter sneered. "You'll shit in your hat, too, Lutie Trask. Kid's a good name, all right. Hell, we're nothin' but kids. Jake an' Petey Quinn only sixteen, you an' me a year older, an' my kid brother, Jimmy not turned fifteen. Bubba Horton there's big, but he's a month shy of fourteen. The rest ain't much older. How'er we gonna build this reputation?"

"By robbin' and killin', you dumb fuck," Luther Trask yelled.

Then he cut a sidelong glance at Jimmy Cutter. Big, deep-blue eyes stared from under silken lashes, a small, sweetly smiling mouth, cotton-top kid with a light gold color to his skin. Jake had become difficult of late. He was more in the way than a help. Maybe he should look elsewhere for a best friend. Kid Trask dropped his line of speculation at a faint sound from off around the bend. He made a quiet signal to the others.

There it came again . . . the soft clop-clop of horses' hoofs. Two, maybe three. Kid Trask nodded in satisfaction and pointed. His words came in a whisper. "There come our first customers."

"How can you be so sure?" Jake asked, still stinging from Luther's apparent rejection. "This trail ain't traveled much."

"Which gives us more time to strip our victims clean," the Kid growled. "Now hush up. They'll be in sight in a minute."

Two figures appeared first, as they rounded the bend and kept to the overgrown ruts of the trace. A packhorse, on a lead, came behind. Kid Trask watched them come nearer. One of them had long, black braids, he noted. A man and a woman, perhaps? No matter, they would be the first they robbed.

"Spread out," the Kid commanded in a hoarse whisper. "Wait until they get almost to that lone pine there. Then we open up."

Chapter 14

"We'll stop and eat a bit when we get out of these rocks," Rebecca suggested as she and Aaron rode along the track they had followed.

Rounding a bend, they encountered a long, straight stretch bordered by more scattered boulders; they looked as though a giant's children had abandoned a game of marbles, Rebecca mused. Far above, a hawk skreed and began to plummet toward some hapless rodent or reptile. Neither Rebecca nor Aaron had said any more about the undefined situation in the valley of holy pilgrims, yet Aaron could not stop worrying it in his mind.

Rebecca's intuition bothered him all the more as they rode along the trail, so much so it caused him to speak testily. "So what should we have done? Stayed around and found out about their secret?"

"No, of course not. It isn't our business," Rebecca answered sharply, set on edge by his flash of temper and an odd sensation of unbalance in their surroundings.

Nature might as well have abandoned them, she thought. There, that was it. No birds chirped or warbled, even the insects seemed to have gone to ground. Only the lone hawk. Not a breath of air stirred. All her old, Sioux-born instincts shouted *danger*. She started to comment on it when the first shot cracked through the stillness.

"What—!" Aaron blurted, his hat knocked askew by

the passing bullet, which holed the crown only a fraction of an inch above the top of his head.

Rebecca didn't bother to state the obvious; that someone was shooting at them. Instead she slid from Śila's back and yanked her Winchester .45-70-600 Express rifle from the scabbard. Compelling the spotted rump stallion to lie down, she took shelter behind its bulk. Her wrist rested on the right stirrup fender, fingers firmly gripped the forestock of her weapon. Taking a deep breath and slowly letting out half, she took aim on the next puff of smoke.

It had no more than appeared when she squeezed off a round. Rebecca's bullet splattered on hard granite, sending up a spray of rock chips and bits of hot lead. Immediately a scream rose from behind and a high, thin voice.

"I'm blind! Oh, God, I can't see, Arlowe. Help me."

"Shut up, Jimmy," came the answering snarl.

Two rifles opened up at once, and another voice, nearly as high as the first commanded, "Let's charge 'em."

In the pause that followed, while the youthful outlaws mounted, a single rifle continued to lay down inaccurate fire. Whimpers and an occasional sob accompanied its bark. Then hoofs drummed and the masked young men appeared from ahead where an enormous boulder masked the trail. At once, Rebecca came to her feet, urged Śila to stand and swung into the saddle. Much to the chagrin of the teen-aged bandits, they quickly found out what a terrible mistake they had made.

With the range closing rapidly, Rebecca switched to her Colt Bisley. The big .45 spat a slug that knocked another masked bandit from his saddle. Swiftly she changed targets to Peter Quinn. A forlorn cry of pain and despair marked his demise. Beside her, Aaron had remounted and sent a bullet into the meaty chest of a chubby young outlaw. Throwing up his hands, the dying youth rolled backward over his horse's rump. Then

Aaron sighted in on the lead horse. His bullet went true, taking the animal in the chest. Long, shaggy locks of curly blond hair streamed in the breeze while the rider did a forward roll over his dying horse's neck and head. With the highwayman's charge blunted, Rebecca exchanged sixgun for rifle and turned her attention to the sniper again.

"Damn you, Luther, damn you to hell," Arlowe Cutter raged inwardly while he levered another round into his Winchester.

With one hand he held a neckerchief over his little brother's eyes in a desperate attempt to staunch the flow of blood. He paused in his doctoring to fire wildly downhill at their intended victims. Then he turned to Jimmy.

Only one eye had been damaged, he noted, a disfigured shard of gray lead protruding from the eyeball. Blood from a dozen cuts on Jimmy's forehead had washed into both sockets, blinding the boy. Arlowe cycled the Winchester again and fired, then grabbed up a canteen. Hands shaking, he uncorked the mouth and gently poured the tepid liquid over Jimmy's face.

"Ow! Oh, Jesus, Arlowe, it hurts like hell," Jimmy keened in a soprano register. "I'll never see again," he wailed, while his small fists pounded the ground.

"Yes you will. Just let me get the blood out of your eyes. Only some cuts on your forehead."

"My eyes feel like there's a pound of hot sand in them," Jimmy panted. His skin had taken on a gray-green pallor.

"Only for a little while," Arlowe assured him.

"Am I gonna die, Arlowe?"

"'Course not, Jimmy. Here, you hold onto this kerchief. Keep it wet and cover your eyes with it."

"Wh-what you gonna do?"

"Go back to shootin' the one who did it to you,"

143

Arlowe said with a confidence he didn't feel.

Cautiously he raised up and took aim. Down the slope he saw a puff and the thin stream of gray that enlarged into a dense puff. Funny, he mused, it was almost like he was looking directly down the barrel of that one's gun. He blinked his eyes to banish the illusion an instant before Rebecca Caldwell's six-hundred-grain .45-70 slug struck the center of his forehead and blew what little brains he had out the back of his head.

Jake Ramsey saw Luther Trask's horse take a spill and cut in close beside his dearest friend. "Oh, please don't let anything happen to him," he prayed aloud to a god whose name and nature he knew nothing about.

In no time it seemed he flashed past the thrashing, dying horse. Bent low, an arm crooked and extended, he came alongside the stunned Luther. "Kid—Kid! Here, take my arm," he yelled in the confusion of gunfire and thudding hoofs.

Luther came to his feet with alacrity and put out his own arm. Jake made the pick-up and Luther swung aboard. He landed hard on the skirt of the saddle, atop the surging rump of Jake's horse.

"Ow! My balls," he bleated.

"Don't worry about them now," Jake cried in relief. "We're in trouble."

"I know it. Shoot that bitch. Shoot her!" he shouted.

Ahead of them Jake saw Rebecca taking aim into the rocks. The big Express rifle bucked and spewed smoke. A moment later hideous shrieks came from the rocks. Uttering a demented howl, Jimmy stood upright, exposing himself. He was dripping with blood and bits of shiny gray matter.

"Arlowe, oh, God, Arlowe! He—he's all over meeeeee!" Jimmy began to gag and bent double to vomit. Aaron's bullet, meant for the boy, snapped through empty air above Jimmy's back.

"They're killin' him, they're killin' Jimmy," Luther howled, a note of protectiveness unnatural to the vicious young criminal clear in his voice. "Rein to the right, *to the right!*"

"What'er you doin'?" Jake asked in panic.

"Get between 'em. Keep Jimmy safe. I don't wanna—wanna lose him now."

Horrified, Jake turned to shriek in Luther's face. *"What about us?* Those bullets will kill us just as dead."

Luther ignored him. One hand cupped to his mouth he bellowed, "Jimmy! Jimmy, get down." Reaching forward, he grabbed the reins from Jake.

"Oh, God, God, we're gonna die," Jake wailed.

Aaron's next bullet proved him nearly right. It smashed into his sternum and sent a shower of bone shards to slash his lungs. Stunned, his mind blanked by shock, Jake slumped forward over the pommel of his saddle, his cheek against the sweaty neck of his horse. Howling maniacally, Luther drew his left-hand Model '60 and popped two fast caps at Aaron. The flat-base conical slugs went wide of the mark, yet close enough to throw off Aaron's aim. A gurgling sound came from Jake's blood-foamed mouth. Heedless of the implied obligation, Luther used his left hand to free Jake's legs and callously threw his young friend off the surging, grunting mount. Stark terror brought unsettling questions to his mind.

How could it have gone so wrong? Could they have made a mistake? Who were these people? Jimmy . . . is he all right? Oh, Jimmy, so sweet, so innocent. His heart swelled with affection as images of Jimmy Cutter rose in his mind. Suddenly he saw clearly what had to be done.

Fully in the saddle now, Luther swerved once again, headed directly for the two people they planned to rob and kill. Smoke streamed from the percussion revolver again and again as he rode down his enemy. The loud, meaty smack caught him by surprise as he had a second horse shot out from under him. Howling in frustrated rage, Luther went flying, the Remington dislodged from his hand.

In the wild confusion of the deadly encounter the three remaining outlaws outdistanced Luther and flung themselves in between Rebecca and Aaron. One of them pressed in close, intent on firing point blank into Rebecca's breast. Trained as a war pony, the big Palouse, Sila, bugled in outrage and rose on his hind quarters. His powerful forehoofs slashed out and downward. Hide tore and blood spurted from the neck of the teenaged outlaw's horse. Sila rose again and his hoofs flashed.

The head of the would-be hardcase popped like an overripe melon. To his left, another delinquent began to choke and gag, pointing to the spherical crimson haze that hovered where his companion's head had once been.

"Gaw—gaw—gawd, look at it," he shrieked. Lashing his mount he sought to break free.

Sila's hoofs cleaved the air again and landed solidly on the youth's back. He bolted forward and the Palouse's hoofs came away dripping blood, a bit of cloth and flesh clinging to one shoe. Back broken, the teenaged robber bounded across the broken ground on his runaway horse, making a crowlike sound with icy lips.

"You baaaastarrrrds!" Luther howled as he began his charge on foot.

Up on his feet again, Luther continued to rush at Rebecca. Believing him unarmed, she forbore shooting the youth. In a flash of time she became stunned by his lack of age. Her left-hand Bisley shot dry, Rebecca holstered it and reached for her other one. At that moment, Luther whipped out his stubby double-action Smith and fired at Rebecca.

Stinging heat and pain tore along the top of her left shoulder. Biting back a cry, she swiftly drew. Luther looked for a moment into the big, black hole before the

146

hammer fell and flame gushed from the .45 Colt Bisley. At once Luther thought he had run into an invisible wall. A powerful blow sent pain through his chest. Merciful numbness followed and he took two more steps, again raising his Smith .44 DA.

Running on reflex and adrenaline, his trigger finger cycled two rapid rounds before a puny report registered on his consciousness, and something slammed him stingingly and hotly in the side of his head. Knocked sideways by a heavy, underpowered slug, Luther staggered in an attempt to keep upright. He fired again.

"Shit!" Aaron blurted, realizing a light powder charge had slipped through inspection. "I hit him in the head. Won't anything kill him?"

"Yes," Rebecca answered simply as a 250-grain .45 slug from her Bisley blew away the tip of Luther's nose and drove his septum into his brain.

"Jesus, is that all of them?" Aaron asked into the sudden silence that descended on the trail.

"A—all except for a little one up there in the r-rocks, A-Aaron," Rebecca answered a bit unsteadily.

Oh, God, she thought. *He can't be any bigger than Joey.* The idea of killing a child tore at her, drew her to the edge of physical sickness. She swallowed rapdily to force back the bile that rose in her throat.

"How little?" Aaron asked, unsure.

"A boy, Aaron. Just a little boy," Rebecca stated, ending on a rising note of self-condemnation.

Aaron spurred his mount into motion. Buck took the incline easily, guiding himself around the jumble of boulders. Aaron came to where Jimmy Cutter knelt beside his brother's corpse. The slightly built boy of fourteen had hands clasped to his face. His shoulders shook with heart-wrenching sobs, and pink-stained tears spilled between severely nail-bitten fingers.

"Arlowe? Arlowe? Say something, Arlowe," Jimmy gulped.

"It's all over, son," Aaron said softly. "He's dead.

147

They all are."

"And it's all your fault," Jimmy raged, bitterness pouring from him like bile. "You did it to 'em. You had no right!"

"You were all trying to kill me and my friend," Aaron reminded the lad.

"Sure, but that's okay. We're—we're desperados. We're supposed to shoot people and rob them."

"And I'm a United States Marshal. It's my job to hang murderers and thieves."

Tears had washed the blood from Jimmy's eyes by the time he looked up at Aaron. His left orb was still gorged with scarlet from the sliver of lead stuck in it, the other a bright, clear blue. "I guess we fucked up, huh? Picked the wrong people to start our robbin' an' killin'?"

"That you did," Aaron answered soberly. "Now come down and answer a few questions about how this all got to happen."

"No, sir. I gotta stay with my brother. He—he needs me."

"We'll take care of him right away. You can walk down there, or I'll carry you."

Jimmy stared at Aaron. Even with the red stain on his coat from the shallow flesh wound in his side, the big lawman looked entirely capable of carrying out his threat. Jimmy gulped. "I'll walk, sir. If it's all right with you."

Rebecca set to treating the boy's eye. She asked his name and he told her in a subdued voice. Her remorse increased as she catalogued the similarities between the slim little lad and her stepson, Joey Ridgeway. "There but for the grace . . ." she thought. How little it would have taken to nudge Joey into the life of a criminal when he was in puberty-induced rebellion. With a shiver she shook off the compelling emotions and tended her patient.

Using the magnifying glass from the tiny sewing kit in her saddlebag, along with a strong set of tweezers from the same source, she located and removed the sliver of lead from Jimmy's eye. He uttered only a small whimper when she tightened the jaws of the steel tool on the slippery metal and gave a firm tug.

"Now, that wasn't too bad, was it?"

"N-no, ma'am," Jimmy admitted meekly enough.

"I'm going to mix a poultice that will hopefully keep infection from setting in."

"I don' care if it does," said Jimmy in a sullen pout. "Nobody to look after me now. You kilt m'brother, Arlowe. You din't have no right."

"The fact that he was trying to kill me doesn't mean anything to you?" Rebecca burst out in frustration.

Jimmy's expression reflected utter incomprehension. "What if he was? We runned away from our folks, 'cause they kept tryin' to make us do things we didn't want to. Nobody has the right to tell us what to do."

Heartsick, Rebecca completed her task in silence and bound a makeshift patch over Jimmy's eye. She paused then, faintly conscious of the distant pounding of hoofs. Her gaze went to their back-trail, then returned to the sulky boy seated on a rock.

"How many of you attacked us?" Rebecca demanded.

"Eight. Just eight of us," Jimmy answered readily.

"You're sure, Jimmy? You wouldn't be omitting a few who are riding in now to close the trap?"

"Ain't no more, lady, I tol' you that."

Rebecca sighed and turned away to study on the unknown menace rapidly approaching them. How could something so uncomplicated as childhood go so terribly wrong? What made self-centered, child criminals like this completely devoid of morality or decency? *Bad seed:* the term came to her from the dim past of her childhood, when an aunt from back east had come visiting the Caldwell homestead in Nebraska. Three centuries ago, a boy like Jimmy would have been called "possessed" and burned at the stake to free him of the demon within. How horrid. Yet was there any cure for the amoral, hate-

149

driven children of rage?

Her reflections on the newly emerging subculture of youthful criminals ended when she got a brief, three-second glimpse of four riders in the distance, rounding the first switchback and headed for the bend in the trail that led to where she and Aaron waited.

"Aaron, we've got company coming. Make sure all the weapons are reloaded."

"More trouble?" Aaron inquired.

"It might be. No reason to take chances."

"I hope it is, I hope they kill you both," Jimmy blurted in a nasty, spiteful tone.

Aaron reached the boy in three steps, hot anger flaring as he grabbed Jimmy's shoulder. "You may have a hurt eye, but that don't keep me from warming your rump. Get this straight in your head: I cut no slack for snot-nosed, filthy-mouthed brats. I'd as leave bring you in wrapped in a slicker and layin' across a saddle as look at you."

For the first time, Jimmy paled markedly. His jaw trembled, and tears started from his eyes. Only his lower lip, thrust out in a defiant pout, revealed the hard core of inhumanity in his breast. Before Aaron could make good his threat of a spanking, the mounted men came into sight and the one in the lead raised an arm to signal friendly intent. When they came nearer, Rebecca recognized them as men from the religious community they had left the previous morning. In the lead was Hagar Olaf.

"*Ja,* sure, it's good we catch up with you," Hagar greeted them. His eyes went wide when he took in the litter of corpses. "You baine having a fight?"

"That we did. Would-be highwaymen," Aaron informed him. "All dead but this one."

"What brings you after us?" Rebecca asked.

"Father Asmodeus sent us. He is one worried fella, *ja,* sure. He says for us to tell you the truth and ask that you return with us."

"I'm sorry, we have business to attend to in Flagstaff," Rebecca said.

Frowning, Aaron held up a hand to forestall her dismissal. "Let's hear what they have to say. You said yourself that you were curious as to what was behind their strange behavior."

"All right, Aaron," Rebecca accepted dubiously. "What's this all about?"

"The Congregation of Heavenly Pilgrims is a peaceable sect," one of the older men explained. "As such, we have no means of protecting ourselves from men of violence, or vicious animals. Although we must condemn your methods, it appears you have already eliminated one potential threat to our peace and serenity," he added, looking around.

"The fact is we have another very real, dangerous challenge the True One has sent to us," he continued, "one we must frankly admit we have been unable to defeat with prayer. I understand that the woman," he nodded toward Rebecca, "heard mention of the 'demon beast.' I assure you it is quite genuine, not a figment of the imagination. We know it to be some sort of predatory animal that has been raiding our flocks and livestock. It has also killed a man and a child. Both were alone at the time and we have no idea what sort of creature it might be. Father Asmodeus urged us to appeal to you, to beg if necessary, that you come back and track down this monster, be it demon or living flesh."

"I don't really see what benefit it would be for us to return to your valley," Rebecca protested. "Surely you men can build some sort of snare or trap."

"We did. It broke out of the cage we constructed as though it had been made of paper," another pilgrim admitted with embarrassment.

"It's a terribly powerful beast," a third added.

"Who knows what bloody deeds it might do if you don't stop it, *ja* sure," Hagar contributed, his gaze fixed worshipfully on Rebecca.

151

"I—we, that is . . ." Rebecca stopped and turned to Aaron. His expression gave scant help, but he did make a small, affirmative nod. Sighing, Rebecca faced their petitioners.

"We can't spend the rest of our lives doing this. There's scant time to do anything at all. Aaron favors it, so we will come and make an effort. You have to agree that if it turns out to be an animal or a deranged man, we will kill it and face no penalty under your religious laws."

"No—no, nothing like that," the delegation hastened to assure.

Rebecca sighed resignedly. "All right. Let's get these bodies buried and we'll start back."

"What about me?" Jimmy complained with a whine. "I'll not go anywhere with you. You don't know what sort of danger there might be for me."

"You are not a part of our considerations," Aaron told him coldly.

"You can't make me go," Jimmy sniveled. "You have no right . . ."

"Your favorite expression," Rebecca said bitterly. "All right, you can have your way. We can leave you here, alone, unarmed, wounded, and let you find out what sort of danger might come your way."

His good eye darting nervously in its socket, Jimmy gulped back his selfish defiance and uttered a tiny whine. "I gotta have a horse."

"We'll get one," Rebecca snapped. "One of you ride ahead and tell your, ah, pastor we're coming behind."

Chapter 15

For three days, war drums had throbbed in the Shoshone village of Walks Around. Spirited young men from other Shoshone bands far and wide rode in daily to swear allegiance to the war leaders, Walks Around and Red Shirt. Before they launched their grand attack against Big Mac Kellog and his loggers, hundreds of warriors and their families would swell the encampment to bursting. Walks Around stood watching these events, arms folded over his chest, ceremonial bonnet riffling in the breeze, his face lined and somber. A great shout went up from the western edge of the busy community, and Walks Around looked in that direction.

A moment later the camp crier came forward, lance uplifted. "The Utes come from the land of sand. Many lances, many bows. They come to fight. The Utes come."

"Make them welcome in my name," Walks Around gave the ritual answer. "Ask which war leader they chose to follow."

"They come wearing red shirts," the herald announced.

"So be it. My son will be pleased."

With the sun two finger widths above the horizon, all of the food and preparations had been completed for a grand feast. Children ran shouting, their faces and hands shiny with grease as they snatched tidbits to sample the roasted meat and bubbling stewpots of dog. The big drum sounded and the people gathered to eat.

"There will be a big going to war against the whites," several of the hate-fired young men shouted as the meal progressed.

It well suited the Utes, who had always been white-haters. The drumming and singing began while the revelers drank coffee with lots of sugar and nibbled on the first of spring's berries. Aloof from the others, seated in a place of honor, the war chiefs and council discussed the course of what would follow.

"There are many who will be disappointed," Walks Around observed. "They come thinking to make war on all whites."

"That would be a bad thing," a council chief from the far off Duchesne River country agreed. "But part of me asked, 'Why not?'"

"Our people are at peace with the whites, you know this," Walks Around responded. "Although sometimes I wonder. Did we somehow give in too easily to an accommodation with the white-eyes?"

"We may never know," another wise old man stated flatly.

Red Shirt snorted. "What you mean is, we may never live long enough to find out."

"Your son is full of fire," Two Elks contributed.

"It is his oldest son, his favorite, who is still captive to the tree cutters. Our fight is to get him back."

Anger suffused the face of Lieutenant Colonel Jeremy Alford. The paper on his desk offered no possible alternative explanations. Written by the resident agent on the southern Shoshone reservation, and accompanied by a declaration by Walks Around, the band's chief, the story of a cowardly, bloody-handed massacre of women, children, and old people could not be accepted as anything else. Appended to the agent's report was a private communication informing Alford that a large war

154

party was gathering at the summer hunting camp. He, the agent, and his ten Indian police and detachment of twenty-four green troops were powerless to do anything about it. Lieutenant Colonel Alford swiftly reviewed his options and crossed the room to the door.

"Sergeant, send for Lieutenant Koenig at once."

"Yes, sir," the noncom responded.

Three minutes later, the young officer reported to his commander. He stood stiff and proper before the desk. His clear, blue eyes and boyish features belied the fact that he had been a first lieutenant for five years. For all that, Lieutenant Colonel Alford felt painfully aware of the difference in their ages.

"Sit down, Koenig," Lieutenant Colonel Alford invited.

"Thank you, sir." A good soldier and capable leader, Matthew Koenig knew better than to ask the purpose of the summons.

"I want you to read these and give me your opinion," the post commander instructed as he handed Koenig the reports.

Matt Koenig read swiftly. He began to frown after the first paragraph. By the completion of it, he had become agitated. "I'm no Indian-lover, sir, but from the nature of these reports, I'd say something has to be done about it."

"Right you are, Lieutenant. And it's going to be up to you to handle it. Who do you feel is at fault?"

"This man Kellogg, of course," Lieutenant Koenig answered without hesitation. "He or someone working for him. Making an unprovoked attack on a peaceful village is just asking for a general uprising. These men have to be stopped."

"Precisely. Therefore, I'm ordering you to take a platoon into the field, locate the white men responsible for the massacre of peaceful Indians in the Shoshone village, and arrest them. Send them back here, in chains and under guard, and then remove the Shoshone to their proper reservation. Also any other Indians who might be

155

in their camp at the time. I know they're supposed to be able to hunt down in the area from Marble Canyon to the Tonalea Basin at this time of the year. Seeing the whites actually put under arrest will help, and moving them out of this country for a while should insure a satisfactory solution. Ah—don't forget to get names and descriptions of those who are willing to testify against the offending whites."

"As you wish, sir," Lieutenant Koenig responded. "Anything else, sir?"

"Matt, there's no guarantee, of course, but if you pull this off, I think I can get you that other bar this time around. *Captain* Koenig would sound pretty good, don't you think?"

Matthew Koenig's chest swelled. "Quite good, sir. But I'd do my utmost on this mission without any inducement. We have enough problems without some idiot stirring up the tribes. And any man who makes war on women and children is a bastard in my books, anyhow. One thing, though, Colonel. What if the Shoshone and their allies have already set out on the warpath?"

Alford frowned and vigorously rubbed his chin. "That's where we—ah—have to split some mighty fine hairs, Matt. The way I call it, so long as they don't harm anyone not directly involved in hurting them, we don't see anything the Shoshone do."

Koenig beamed. "That makes my job half as difficult as I expected it to be, sir. I'll contact Sergeant Hammond and have the troops ready to depart within an hour."

"I appreciate the zeal. But make it tomorrow morning, Matt. You'll be gone some while, and you'll need time to prepare supplies."

Riding single file, Father Asmodeus's delegation entered the valley of the Congregation of Heavenly Pilgrims with Rebecca Caldwell and Aaron Hawkins. Its serenity now seemed overlaid with dark foreboding. Even the sheep seemed subdued over their last visit here, Rebecca considered. Impatient with herself for agreeing to come, she insisted they go at once to Father Asmodeus. They found the religious leader at the Temple.

He came out to greet his press-ganged deliverers. Elder Perkins and Deacon Danner stood at his sides. "May the peace of the True One be with you," he said by way of benediction.

"Father Asmodeus, we have a prisoner who must be confined before we get on with this," Aaron Hawkins announced.

Asmodeus furrowed his brow. "He will not be confined. None are prisoner in this valley of peace," he intoned pontifically.

Aaron stood his ground. "Not this murderous, ambushing son of a b—" Biting off his words, he took a deep breath and continued. "Either he gets locked up, or we leave right this minute."

"Very well. We have a—ah—a reflection chamber. It is a place for those who err and are in need of silence and solitude to contemplate their sins. Perhaps it would do?" Asmodeus proposed, without the slightest indication of hypocrisy.

"Good. So long as it will hold the little hellion," Aaron agreed.

"The walls are of seasoned hardwood, three feet thick. There are no windows, only a peep-hole in the door. The ceiling is fifteen feet high, made of timbers with native stone over them, and the floor is of foot-thick blocks of quarried granite."

"A solitary cell, eh? What a cozy place. Too bad you don't have a proper jail, with bars and bunks and windows."

Apparently Aaron's sarcasm was missed by Asmodeus. "But that would be in contradiction to our vow of no violence. Men of the True One were not meant to be kept in cages like animals."

"No—no, of course not," Aaron skirted on satire.

157

"Tell us about these mysterious deaths," Rebecca interjected to prevent a more scathing performance by Aaron.

"Ah, yes. Most unfortunate. Something unnatural—ah—supernatural has attended in each case. You see, the victims, both animal and human, had been disemboweled and almost drained of their blood. It was as though someone in league with Satan was feeding his dreadful master."

"As I said to the men you sent after us, keep the religious mumbo-jumbo out of it," Rebecca stated harshly. "Did you find any physical evidence at the site of the killings?"

"Nothing. Some scratch marks in the ground, not much blood. It was usually hours before anyone noticed the missing animals or people."

Privately, Rebecca wondered how that could be in so tightly controlled a community. "I see. Then I suggest the first thing we do is check the areas where killings have taken place."

After examining three locations, Rebecca and Aaron compared their findings. "An animal of some sort," Aaron suggested.

"Definitely. I suspect a large mountain lion," Rebecca contributed.

"He'd have to be big," Aaron enlarged. "And damned dangerous if he's started going after people. Usually they won't attack a person unless cornered, or protecting young."

"I don't know . . . I'm not sure, anyway, but I haven't any indication it's a female," Rebecca disputed.

"Perhaps one that has been lamed or injured?" she added at the fourth site. "See the drag marks and the gouges from unretracted claws?"

Aaron looked admiringly at her. "I would have missed that. I think you're right. Let's go back and tell the good Father."

Rebecca looked quizzically. "I'm no more convinced

of his holiness than you are, Aaron. But I think a little less of your cynicism would be healthy around here."

"Agreed."

Father Asmodeus heard their report in brooding silence. "You have done remarkably well," the religious leader complimented them. "Considering how long ago some of those terrible attacks happened, it's a wonder you came up with anything."

"We started at the most recent and worked backward," Rebecca informed him.

"I . . . see. What do you propose now?"

"We go out and look for your killer cat," Aaron offered.

Hagar Olaf had been hovering around Rebecca through the entire preliminary investigation. Now he came forward, his big, round, flat face beaming. "*Ja*, sure, and I will go along."

Rebecca and Aaron looked at each other and back to Hagar. "It's going to be extremely dangerous, Hagar," Aaron advised.

"That's hokey-dokey. I can look out for myself."

"How? If you won't carry a gun and use it to protect yourself or others, why go after a killer cat? How can you be of any use in a case like that?"

Hagar pulled a face like a small boy caught in the molasses barrel. He hadn't begun an answer when a loud, panicked shout from the edge of the community attracted everyone's attention.

A woman came running and screaming toward them, tears flowing freely down her face. So distraught was she that her words lacked coherence. Patiently Father Asmodeus calmed her. He hugged her close and patted her head like that of a small child when she gulped her way out of the grip of hysteria.

"All right, Sarah, it's all right now. Tell us what happened."

"A great, golden beast, the demon beast, came at the children."

"What do you mean?"

"Father Asmodeus, you know that spot where the children go to fish and the, ah, backsliders among the boys go to swim? The beast came not twenty minutes ago. It captured a small girl, little Leah Thomas, strayed a bit away. I heard her screams. It was awful. Then this monster growled and roared. When I found her, Leah had been savagely mauled. Her head was crushed and huge teeth had pierced her chest. There was—no blood anywhere."

Both hands covering her eyes, she began to sob. Rebecca said over the poor woman's bowed back, "Aaron, let's get down there right away."

Within minutes, they determined that the attacker was indeed a mountain lion, one the size of a Bengal tiger. Disturbingly, they found no sign of the mutilated child, and the huge pug marks caused the woman to go into another fit of hysterics. Rifles ready in hand, Rebecca and Aaron paced out several dozen yards in every direction. Rebecca spotted something at once.

"There, he took off to the south. I'm sure of it. Blood drops beside the pug marks. Get the horses, and we'll set out at once."

"You wished to see me, Brother Hagar?" Asmodeus asked when the blond giant entered the small office in one wing of the temple.

"Yes, Father Asmodeus. You know that for all the time I am here I'm without a woman. And the Book of Hours says that men must cleave to woman and produce children for the greater glory of the True One. Now, I— I . . ."

Amused at this simpleton, Asmodeus smiled, hoping his expression would be taken as encouragement and sympathy. "You have found the woman you wish to take as your own?"

"*Ja*, sure, that's the truth of it, Father. She is most

beautiful. But she can be taught to be plain, as befits a woman," he hastened to add. Then, lowering his eyes and his voice, he confessed his weakness. "She is not one of us. She lives in terrible sin, wearing the clothing of men and—and such sinful things," Hagar stammered out.

"I see," Asmodeus made ritual response, though he didn't quite see at all.

"In the Book of Hours it says a person can come to holiness only through accepting the one true faith. If she is instructed in our ways and given to me as my woman, she will be purified. *Ja,* sure. Isn't that the way it is?"

"Ummmm. That is somewhat oversimplified. But it is more or less what we believe."

Hagar brightened, relief displayed on his face like the sun emerging from a storm cloud. "Then all I need is your permission and I can take her as my own."

Asmodeus arched an eyebrow. "You haven't even told me her name. How can I permit it if I don't know the woman involved."

Taken aback by this, Hagar stammered, "Oh—ah—but I—I thought . . . ? *Ja,* sure, it's the beautiful black-haired girl who goes to kill the demon beast."

Father Asmodeus nodded knowingly. "Rebecca Caldwell lives with violence like a mother with a babe at her breast," he said coldly. "It will take great faith to save her from herself. Are you such a man, Hagar Olaf?"

Hagar's chest swelled, and he thumped a thumb against his bony sternum. "*Ja,* sure, Father Asmodeus, I baine such a man. I will be strong enough for us both." He paused, a frown flickering through his glowing self-confidence. "But what about the black-hearted man she rides with? He stinks of violence and death."

"Not to worry, Hagar," Asmodeus said jauntily, then spoke darkly, "We'll take care of that after the demon beast is slain."

Chapter 16

Constantly moving upward into rugged country, Rebecca and Aaron noted that the pug marks revealed increasing difficulty the huge cat had had in carrying its own weight and that of the small child it had carried off. Unquestionably aware of pursuit, the killer cougar had not holed up close to its kill as usual, but had chosen to drag it off. Caution kept the hunters to a pace nearly as slow as that of their prey.

"He could be anywhere," Aaron surmised after the second hour. "There are overhangs and clefts all through these mountains."

"Not too far from the valley," Rebecca said. "Considering his condition, he couldn't have ranged too widely from his lair."

Aaron marvled at the unsuspected aspects of this young woman he had come to love. He had so far taken each revelation in stride. Compounded, their effect startled him. Unlike any woman of his past acquaintance, she remained ever so cool under fire, was deadly accurate with any firearm, and had a horse that fought like the fabled chargers in the days when knighthood was in flower. She could track men or animals, cook fantastic meals over a campfire, and make love with all the consummate skill of a harem favorite. It prompted him to pry into the reasons.

"Someday you're going to have to tell me about it."

"About what, Aaron?" Rebecca asked.

"How you got to be so proficient at . . . almost everything."

"I—the time has to be just right for that," Rebecca told him gently. "Sometimes I don't quite believe all of it myself."

Away from the settled area of the valley, the trees soon increased in number. They rode in under ancient, scarred trunks with huge boughs hanging over the track they followed. Hardly more than a game trail, the winding path drew them further into the forest, always higher. For some while the sign they followed dwindled to an occasional scrape or a partial paw print. Aaron began to think they would ultimately lose their quarry and have to return and devise some plan to lure the man-killer to them.

"This ground's getting so hard, I think we're going to lose him," Aaron spoke his opinion aloud.

"What? Giving up so easily?" Rebecca taunted.

They approached one giant fir, with thigh-thick lower branches that stretched out thirty and forty feet. As they rode under one huge limb, a sudden coughing snarl came from above them. Rebecca and Aaron went rigid with alarm, and their horses whinnied in fright. Between heartbeats, the cougar leaped at Rebecca.

Liquid gold flashed through the air, and one big paw knocked Rebecca sideways. The feral cat whirled and thrashed in the air and hooked claws into cloth to drag Rebecca from her horse. Snarling in fury and its own pain, the abnormally large mountain cat sought to position its hind feet for the fatal disemboweling slashes. Rebecca screamed once, a short, strident cry. Aaron stared on, helpless.

In a flurry of legs, arms and growling feline head, he had no way to safely shoot. Over and over Rebecca and the cougar rolled down the slope. In the moment after the first painful contact, panic and defeat seized Rebecca's mind. Then she and the beast struck the ground. It jolted her mind into an aggressive mode, and she began to resist. Twisting to protect her vulnerable abdomen from the churning kicks of the hind feet, she held the cougar's long, yellowed fangs away with a stranglehold. When the rolling began, the animal instinctively tucked its head in to avoid injury.

That freed one of Rebecca's hands. The mountain lion's forepaws embraced her like a lover, preventing her from reaching her holstered .45 Bisleys. Still she had a fragment of hope. Worming her loose arm under the snarling cat's left front leg, she slid downward to the small purse she wore like an old-time mountainman's "possibles bag." She had nearly forced open the puckered mouth when their downhill revolutions ended with a fierce impact against the trunk of a slender pine.

Having taken the brunt of the powerful blow on its back, the cougar lay momentarily stunned. Desperately, Rebecca dug into her beaded buckskin pouch and closed fingers around the gracefully curved grip of her .38 Smith & Wesson Baby Russian. Twisting the muzzle upward, she yanked back the hammer and squeezed off a round. In rapid succession she emptied all five rounds into the deadly animal's chest. Blood soaked her clothing, and its metallic odor overpowered the feline stench of the killer cat. Exerting all her strength, Rebecca broke free before convulsions seized the cougar.

She stumbled when she attempted to rise, and drew her skinning knife from its belt sheath. With a swift, sure stroke, she cut the wounded predator's throat and leaped back. Stifling a sob of relief, she began the steep climb to the game trail.

"Aaron . . . oh, God, I didn't think I could do it," she panted.

Astonished, Aaron Hawkins could only stare. "Y-you killed it," he said wonderingly. "H-here I sat without making a move, and you killed it."

Looking embarrassed, Rebecca lifted her belt purse,

the deerskin leather still smoldering from the repeated muzzle blast that had ignited it. "I'll have to get a new one," she said lamely.

"Do you want to tell me the rest of it? Tell me how it is you are so good with firearms and how you can kill the biggest cougar I've ever seen practically bare-handed?"

Her adrenaline rush was dwindling. Rebecca sighed heavily. "We might as well make camp right here. We'll want to skin that beast and take the hide back. Also, that little girl's body should be around here somewhere. And yes, I'll tell you. At least some of it."

Aaron dismounted and rigged hobbles for both horses in a grassy glade beyond the tree that had hidden the mountain lion. He got out his canteen and took a long swallow, sighed, and sat upon a rock.

"All right, what about . . . all of this?" Aaron waved a hand in the direction of the dead cougar.

Suddenly shy, Rebecca spoke disjointedly. "You're . . . a lawman, Aaron, and I . . . don't know how you'll . . . feel about this. You're also a white man, and I don't expect you to fully understand," she blurted. "You see, since I got away from the Sioux, I've been a manhunter. No reason to go into details, it's just . . . what I am."

"But I do want the details," Aaron insisted, rising. "For me, not for Deputy Marshal Hawkins. Please, Becky," he urged as he sat down again and pushed up the brim of his hat.

Rebecca sighed, bit at her lower lip, and continued. "For six years, from the age of fourteen, I was raised among the Oglala. My mother was white, my father was Iron Calf, a war chief of the Red Top Lodge band. We were not there voluntarily." Started now, she quickly told of the involvement of her uncles, Ezekial and Virgil, with the Bitter Creek Jake Tulley Gang and the betrayal that put her mother, Hannah, and herself in the clutches of the Sioux. She omitted reference to her love affair and marriage to Four Horns and the child they had.

She did emphasize the intertribal warfare in which she

learned to defend herself. Then she related her long odyssey to bring retribution to those who had brought grief and suffering to her mother and herself. She told Aaron of her growing proficiency with all manner of weapons and her skills at tracking and outguessing outlaws. That brought her to Roger Stiles and the events leading to his death at her hands. Then, briefly, she brought up Chris Starret.

"It was after Chris and Roger fled to Texas from Guanajuato in Mexico that the events happened I told you about earlier. Chris is still at large and, I'm sure, bringing misery to someone somewhere."

"Then you're going to Flagstaff, expecting to track him down?"

A rueful grin softened Rebecca's strained features. "Yes, I suppose I am. I figured that if he had been causing trouble for the Shoshone before, which he had last fall, he might be again."

For a long while Aaron said nothing. He stared off into the distance, looked at Rebecca and then away, and shook his head in bafflement. At last he sighed heavily, clapped his hands on his thighs, and rose.

"We'd better get camp set up. I, for one, could use a good meal."

"You're not . . . ? I mean, what about—?"

"You and I? I must admit I'm astonished, Becky. I had no idea of what your past had been like. It's unsettling, of course—"

Bitterness colored her words as Rebecca interrupted him. "But you prefer your women far more shy and retiring, more *civilized*. Believe me, Aaron, I had no intention of deceiving you, only in avoiding too graphic a look into my past."

Realization of her intentions wrought a big change in Aaron's expression and his mood. "Now damn it all, Becky, I don't want my women cosseted and out of touch with reality. I need a girl who can ride fork-legged and not cry about what it does to her reputation, one who doesn't swoon every time a gun goes off, and can catch a fish or shoot a deer for the supper table. I want a girl who used to swim bare-butt when she was a little girl and still likes to do it. One who doesn't think making love is a terrible punishment God condemned women to endure, and isn't horrified at the sight of a man's naked body. In other words, Becky Caldwell, I like you just the way you are."

It had been quite a speech. It left Aaron more than a little surprised at his vehement garrulity. In the silence that followed, he reached out with both hands, a pleading gesture. With a gasp of rising hope, Rebecca rushed into his arms.

"Umm. That's more like it," Aaron murmured. "Now let me tell you something. I've got rather definite plans for tonight."

"What sort of plans?" Rebecca asked playfully.

"You'll see. I'll make certain that you're the first to know. Now, you're all covered with blood from that cat. I happened to notice that about a mile back on the trail there's a nice, deep pool at the bottom of a little waterfall. What say we skin out that cat, then go there and get you cleaned up and into some fresh clothes?"

"I find that suggestion impossible to refuse," Rebecca said cheerfully. "Now kiss me, you terrible man."

Aaron darted his head back a few inches and peered at her down his nose. "Only if you kiss me first, you shameless woman."

Eleven well-dressed men, diamond stickpins, pinky rings and other emblems of wealth abounding, sat back from the lavish board well satisfied. They had dined on rare roast beef, a suckling pig, and a bountiful harvest of vegetable dishes. Cheeses, fruit, and a crusty french bread made the rounds now, along with decanters of port, madeira, and brandy. As resplendent as any of his guests, Chris Starret rose and addressed his Phoenix suckers.

"Gentlemen, I trust you appreciated the humble

efforts of the hotel staff in preparing this meal. For all their excellence, they fall short of the dining car complement we intend to have aboard the weekly passenger run to Flagstaff and back. All goes well with the spur. Engineers are drawing up the plans for the roadbed. Everything now hinges on the Santa Fe Board of Directors. I will be going to their eastern terminus in Chicago within a week to present our proposal."

"Here, here!" several voices cried out in praise.

"When I do . . . when I meet with these moguls of the iron horse, I certainly hope to take with me a bank statement that reflects the eager, willing participation of the astute merchants in Phoenix. I came down here from Flagstaff for that express purpose. It wouldn't do for them not to find us financially sound and prepared to expand with the increase in trade this spur represents. Can I count on you gentlemen for generous contributions to that greatest of all convincers, a sound financial statement?"

"What do you need, Starret?" a portly banker brayed. "Hell, my bank can probably float any deficiency in your prospectus."

"What, and cut the rest of us out of the opportunity of a lifetime?" a noted hotelier countered hotly.

"Andrew's right. We all want in on this," the owner of three prosperous saloons injected. "Now I don't want you fellows to take this wrong, understand. But, sometimes, only once in a while, I'm sort of sorry there's quite this many involved. Kind of spreads the profit a bit thin, don't you see?"

"Come now, Edwin," Chris chided, enjoying his role as benefactor. "There'll be plenty for everyone. With a little water, anything will grow around Phoenix. Once we've got the spur in, we can develop an irrigation company, set up township boomer companies, and move in all sorts of settlers. With transportation to the main line through Flagstaff, their farm products will have a ready market. We get rich twice, selling the right of way land and hauling the produce grown on it."

"You make it sound mighty attractive," Andrew relented.

"And easy," another of Chris's pigeons added.

"It's not easy," Chris corrected, setting the hook. "Nor will our way of milking the greatest profit be entirely legal—at least in the eyes of some fancy eastern lawyer. That's one reason we want to see that only those we can trust, the men in this room, are a part of it all. How about it, gents? Can I receive your bank drafts today?"

"You can start with me," one man yelled. "And me!" another cried out. "Here, me, too."

Grinning in satisfaction, Chris sat back down to receive the anxious and voluntary tribute of his happy marks.

Long and white, the feathery plume of water descended sixty feet from the hard granite lip of the higher creek bed. It plunged with deep gurgles into a crystal pool with an emerald bottom. Sunlight sparkled off the surface, dancing on the wavelets that radiated out from the base of the falls.

"I had a place like this at our homestead in Nebraska," Rebecca told Aaron. "Oh, not with the waterfall, but the water was so clear, and a pool had formed behind a sand bar. I used to go there in the summer and swim for hours, then lay naked in the sun and dry off."

"How old were you?" Aaron asked.

"Umm . . . eight, nine, until I was thirteen, actually. I'd be all alone, or sometimes with my friends. They were brother and sister from a neighboring farm."

Aaron began to remove his clothing. Rebecca did the same. She examined the large bloodstains and set the pieces aside for later scrubbing.

"Tell me all about it," Aaron urged.

"You wouldn't want to hear," Rebecca responded, developing a pink tinge.

"Sure I would. *Every* detail."

"You'll think I'm awful."

"No I won't, Becky. I want to know everything there is about Becky Caldwell."

"Well . . . the boy, Bobby, was my age, his sister a year younger. We never thought anything about swimming together buck naked. At eight and nine years old we'd not been taught that much yet about how to be ashamed of our bodies. Only that what we were doing was supposed to be terribly naughty and therefore extremely exciting. I remember Pru—that's Prudence Miller—and I made terrible fun of Bobby for being different than us. Then one day he gave us a big surprise when that little dangle of skin rose right up, stiff as an iron bar. It made Pru jealous. From then on she insisted that we were the ones who got shorted on body parts."

"You weren't bothered?" Aaron asked softly as he removed his underdrawers.

"Not at all. I was fascinated. I thought it was the most wonderful thing I had ever seen in my life. Of course, it wasn't anything as magnificent as this," she added, reaching out to Aaron's rising member.

"Umm . . . I think you were very precocious children," Aaron teased, stepping closer to her.

"We never did anything, ah, serious, Aaron. Pru thought it was all disgusting, wouldn't even look at us. But Bobby and I invented all sorts of fun games built around . . . ummmm. You don't want to hear any more."

"Sure I do," Aaron protested.

"No you don't," Rebecca insisted, cupping him in both her hands. "Let's get in the water and see if you can develop some of those special plans you had in mind."

With a whoop of abandon, Aaron jumped into the pool. The moment his toes touched bottom, he propelled himself upward with enough force that he nearly came completely out of the water. Eyes wide, he slapped stingingly at his goose-bumped skin.

"Wow, that's cold."

"I'll help warm it up," Rebecca offered as she split the surface in a shallow dive. A moment later her head bobbed up, and she spluttered in shocked reaction. "I'm going to freeze," she complained.

"Enough of this," Aaron protested, striking out for the bank. "Get out and we'll find something to do to get us warm again."

"Like what?" Rebecca asked when she joined him on the grassy verge.

Aaron took her forcefully into his arms. "Like this."

Their kiss lasted an eternity. Tongues explored and probed, teased and flirted. Pressed together, the hot length of Aaron's phallus made an indentation in her lower belly. Her breasts made hot, flattened mounds on his chest. Arousal hardened the nipples, and Aaron spared a hand to gently fondle her precious globes. Rebecca began to rub the inside of one leg up and down the outside of Aaron's.

"Now, here, Aaron," Rebecca pleaded with urgency when the embrace ended. "Find a mossy place. It can never be better than right here in this beautiful spot. Hurry. I need you—need you so badly."

Manfully, Aaron sought out their nest and led her to it. There they sank to their knees, kissed longingly, and eased onto their sides. Rebecca encircled his solid shaft and stroked it to a new height of sensitivity. She raised one leg and draped it over his hip. Then he plunged into her cavern of joy, driving to the hilt.

"Ayyyeeee, Aaron, oh, ga-ga-gaaawd, Aaron!" Rebecca wailed.

Mingled energies sustained them as they rocked and shuddered, thrust and withdrew. Above them the birds serenaded, while cheeky squirrels criticized their technique. Memory blended all previous experience into one superlative *now*, and the blood roared in their ears with tidal bore force. Whirled away into a mutual world of absolute pleasure, they reached dizzying heights before the inevitable hurtling through warm, sweet space to a tiny, shared moment of oblivion.

"Oh—do that—do that some more," Rebecca panted when she recovered enough to trust her voice.

"I shall," Aaron reassured her. "I can't seem to get enough of you, Becky. You're more woman than I've ever known. And—and I'm grateful."

"Oh, now, Aaron . . ." Rebecca began to protest.

"No, I mean it. I've never had a vast experience with women," he confessed. "I had a sheltered life. Even though I knew about playing with myself, I was thirteen before I found out there was anything else I could do with it. That took me by considerable surprise. Rather, *she* did, I should say. She was two years older, very knowing, and—more than eager to play the role of teacher. By the time I realized what we were doing, I had visions of burning in hell for eternity. It scared the daylights out of me. I made a mess out of it . . . but only the first time," he concluded with a smug grin.

"Aaah, well, Aaron, they say confession is good for the soul. It appears it's good for something else," Rebecca told him as she wrapped warm, soft fingers around his newly risen member. "You know, I'm quite positive we can find something to do with this."

They did, too . . . until the sun slid out of the sky behind a mountain peak and left them shivering in the lingering twilight.

Chapter 17

Small bells began to tinkle within a minute of when Rebecca Caldwell and Aaron Hawkins topped the rimrock and began to descend into the valley of the holy pilgrims. Herd boys saw them first and set up the high-pitched tintinabulation. Several ran beside them, expressions of fear and wonder mixed on their faces when they saw the golden tail dangling from the tarpaulin bundle on the packhorse. Again Rebecca harkened back to the experiences of her childhood and speculated as to how tough and thorny the soles of their feet must be. Even now "civilized" shoes, like the boots she wore, cramped her toes, and hours of wearing them caused considerable pain. Yet she knew she could walk for miles in a pair of moccasins. They hadn't covered a hundred yards when deeper-toned tocsins took up the heralding from men working their fields.

"Too bad the bells can't tell what we've accomplished," Rebecca said to Aaron.

"They'll know soon enough," he said, a tightness returning to his voice.

"This place really gets to you, doesn't it?" Rebecca observed.

"You don't appear overwhelmed with eagerness to return," Aaron opined dryly.

"We'll get it over with and be on our way."

Father Asmodeus and his congregation had other ideas, they soon discovered when they reached the large square around the temple. It seemed that nearly everyone had turned out to see the results. Asmodeus, dressed in his purple-bordered toga, stood on the steps, an arm raised in greeting, or perhaps benediction, Rebecca considered.

"This is the demon beast?" he asked in ringing tones when Aaron removed the tarp and revealed the hide of the cougar. "You are certain of it?"

"We are," Aaron answered curtly.

"An ordinary cougar will shy away from people," Rebecca undertook to explain. "They rarely attack unless cornered. This one ambushed us. We also found the body of the little girl it carried off. We've returned her for burial."

"Praise be!" Asmodeus declared. "We have been delivered! This is a day of great celebration, brothers and sisters. It is even more a blessed day for the announcement I have the pleasure to make next. By the authority of the Book of Hours, and the True One, our Lord, I am happy to decree the betrothal of Brother Hagar Olaf to this brave young woman, Rebecca Caldwell."

Rebecca's first burst of indignant refusal got drowned out by the cheering of the assembled congregation. Not so the second bellow of outrage. "Like hell I'll marry Hagar, or anyone!"

Ostensibly unaffected by her harsh language and unwomanly demeanor, Father Asmodeus snapped, "You have nothing to say about it. It is already decided."

Boiling with fury, Rebecca wanted to grab the religious leader and shake understanding into him. "*I* am the only one who has a say about it," she informed him hotly. "Neither you nor your sheeplike followers can dictate what I will or won't do."

Asmodeus's visage clouded, the fire of righteous rage—or madness—flickered in his pale, nearly colorless gray eyes. "You are a fallen woman. A sinner. You were watched. Your sin with this man was witnessed. You have violated the canons of this holy community from the moment you first arrived here. Hear the number and manner of your evil ways. You dress like a man. You brazenly look a man in the eye, instead of chastely lowering your eyes in the presence of your natural superiors. You are contentious and you talk back. You bear firearms. You kill. The penalty for each of these is a flogging of a hundred lashes and six months in the Reflection Chamber. Only the waters of the sacred fountain can wash away these sins.

"Repent. Submit to this and be born again into the Congregation of Heavenly Pilgrims, marry the man the True One has ordained to be your husband, and keep the canons of our Book of Hours, and all sins will be forgiven. Even your fellow sinner here will be allowed to go his way in peace."

Anger coalesced with contempt. "I refuse."

Surprise flashed for a moment on Asmodeus's face. "Then you both shall be flogged for sinful copulation and your other sins, one hundred stripes for each offense."

Lips twisted in disgust, Rebecca gave vent to her loathing. "You corrupt hypocrite! You prattle of nonviolence, and endorse the most barbaric of punishments for those who don't please you. I'll remind you of one of your charges: I do carry firearms. And I'm extremely proficient in their use. If you or anyone here makes an effort to stop us leaving, you'll see exactly how well I can employ them. Turn over our prisoner to us at once. We're leaving this unhealthy place, and I advise that you do not send anyone after us."

While she had been speaking, Aaron Hawkins stood spread-legged, his hand on the grips of his .45 Colt Peacemaker. His eyes moved restlessly, marking each point of potential trouble. Now he stepped to the packhorse, slipped the bundled hide off onto the ground, and tenderly removed the slicker-wrapped dead child from the packsaddle.

While he performed these tasks, Asmodeus remained deathly silent. When Aaron made ready to remount, he too asked for the outlaw boy, Jimmy Cutter.

"There is no prisoner here," Father Asmodeus answered with a heavy sigh of indifference. "Alas, someone carelessly left the door to the Reflection Chamber unsecured, and the lad made good his escape. It appears you will be leaving empty-handed." He did not mention that Jimmy's escape had taken the boy no farther than the Temple's monastic chambers, where he was well on the way to becoming Asmodeus's favorite acolyte.

"Another piece of unfinished business," Aaron growled. "I'll be back this way for him . . . with a posse." After Rebecca mounted, he swung into his saddle, gave a final, hard look at the gaping congregation, and they rode swiftly from the square.

From behind them came a thin, plaintive cry. "Please take me with you," Josiah wailed wretchedly.

"Stretch 'em out," Rebecca suggested. "I want to be clear of the valley before noon."

"If we are, we can make Flagstaff by mid-morning tomorrow," Aaron advised.

Rebecca suppressed a shudder. "It won't be soon enough for me."

She and Aaron had not made love on that tense, secretive night after leaving the religious community. They made a dry, cold camp and had held each other close, taking turns at staying awake. Neither of them had delusions about the potential threat the fanatics closest to Father Asmodeus represented.

"There's still . . . something seriously wrong in that place," Rebecca had summed up. "It's more, or maybe I should say worse, than what we discovered so far. You were right about Asmodeus, the original one, I mean. Asmodeus, if I remember, was prince of demons, and ranked with Beelzebub, a prince of Hell. What sort of religion would have a high priest named Asmodeus? The sooner we're far away from this country, the better." They had not discussed it further.

Now, as they topped a steep grade, a large, shallow, bowl-like valley emerged from the thick forest of tall pines and firs. Birch and aspen provided lighter relief from the dark, nearly black sameness of the vast stands of conifers. Near the center of the basin thin ribbons of smoke rose from a multitude of chimneys, and Rebecca made out the rough sprawl of a city in the making.

"It's lovely from here," she remarked to Aaron.

"Almost anyplace is, viewed from enough distance," Aaron informed her. "I visited back East once. While there I had the opportunity of looking at New York City from the Jersey bluffs. For all of its hugeness and mad scramble of people, even *it* looked beautiful."

"Are you saying that Flagstaff is flawed, like the, ah, pilgrims we left yesterday?"

"No. Not necessarily," Aaron assured her. "It is new, rough, raw, a bit lawless. But definitely not marching in lockstep to the tune of some demented religious fanatic. There are more saloons than any other business, a tremendous flock of soiled doves, enough tin-horn gamblers to fill Yuma Territorial Prison, no schools, no churches, and no Ladies' Decency League. Other than those conditions, there's nothing wrong with Flagstaff."

Uncertain of whether Aaron was jesting, Rebecca made no reply. Instead she urged Sila into a light trot and welcomed the enlarged roadway that began almost at once. Nearing the town she saw wagons and horsemen streaming toward the center of commerce on roads and trails that radiated from Flagstaff like spokes in a wheel. Rising dust turned the air over the community golden. At a quarter mile the rasp of saws and tattoo crack of hammers came clearly to her ears. Shrill voices bearing shouts and laughter came from the direction of a large pond to the north of the road.

Drawing closer, Rebecca saw the sun's rays strike highlights off the wet, bare skin of a gaggle of small boys who cavorted in the water. It called to mind her own childhood, and, with a jolt, the somewhat erotic antics of stepson Joey and the Parsons youngsters far off in Texas. For all that, it had a healthier aspect than the lives of those poor people in Walnut Canyon.

"I'll check in with the new mayor and then start organizing my investigation. What do you have in mind, Becky?"

"I think I'll talk to whoever is in command of the army around Flagstaff first. Then I'll decide about taking a hotel room, or moving on to the Indian villages."

For some reason, Fate continued to intervene in the plans made by Rebecca and Aaron. When they reached the army outpost on the edge of town, they discovered the soldiers gone and a housekeeping detail in sole occupancy.

"Where had the troops been sent?" Rebecca asked the gate sentry.

"That's army business," the uncommunicative corporal informed her.

"Isn't there anyone I can talk to? It's about the difficulties with the Shoshone."

"You mean Colonel Alford? Won't do you any good. He's not receiving any visitors."

Rebecca forced herself to smile sweetly through her impatience. "Try him. I think he'll see me."

Shrugging, the corporal gave her a long, hungry look up and down, puckered lips to whistle soundlessly, and turned away, a gleam in his eyes. "Hillyard, keep an eye on these people while I go see the colonel."

He returned in a scant two minutes with a puzzled frown replacing the lustful expression his examination of Rebecca had given him. "He'll see you."

The private stepped aside to allow them to pass. Rebecca and Aaron led their horses to the tie-rail in front of the headquarters building, a one-story log building with, surprisingly, double-hung windows of glass. Inside, the duty sergeant indicated the correct office and returned to his stack of paperwork. Aaron knocked.

"Come in," a baritone rumble sounded within.

Their interview with Lieutenant Colonel Alford took less than five minutes. The troops, they were informed, were in the field. He didn't disclose the reason. Rebecca pressed him for it.

"Does it have anything to do with the unrest among the Southern Arapaho?"

"Umm . . . well, ah, that might be one way of looking at it," Alford equivocated.

"Colonel Alford, I have here a telegram from Lieutenant Arthur Trapp in Wyoming. In it he says that the principal chief of the Northern Shoshone, Shining Horse, made a request of him to engage my offices, for whatever good it might do, to prevent an uprising of their cousins, the Southern Shoshone."

One corner of Alford's mouth turned up in a cynical smile. "How, exactly, do you propose to do that?"

"I don't know. I only got here this morning. I do know what I did to prevent war between the Northern Shoshone and the Arapaho last year."

Alford's eyebrows raised. "I—ah—heard about that. Damned near a general uprising along the frontier in Wyoming. The reports I read said something about the involvement of a white woman. Young Trapp's name came up several times, and an Oglala Sioux woman named—ah—something I can't pronounce in their heathen tongue."

"*Šinaskawin.* I am she," Rebecca told him heatedly.

Alford cleared his throat energetically, his face flushed pink. "I—ah—I suppose I made a faux pas. Let's start over again and you can explain it to me."

Rebecca rewarded him with a big, radiant smile. "I'm certain of having a favorable reception by the Shoshone. Whatever it is riling them can be dealt with and that should be the end of it."

"What's bothering them is Mac Kellogg and his whirlwind logging operation that's cutting down all the trees in the Shoshone hunting grounds. Where the troops have gone, and damned few I've got to spare, is to Kellogg's logging and sawmill camps to shut them down, move the people out of there, and arrest certain individuals responsible for a massacre of Shoshone women, children and old folks."

"What?" Rebecca asked, shocked.

"Happened a few days ago. They raided the village at sunup, burned down nearly everything, killed twenty-five or so, and ran off a lot of horses. Shoshone and their agent claim it was white men working for Kellogg who did it."

"Do you have an Shoshone speakers among your troops?"

"Uh—well, there's one or two. Civilian scouts, actually."

"I can't speak the language, but I know I can help identify the ones indicated by the Shoshone. When your men make those arrests, I want to be there. Tell me which way we should go."

Quickly Alford gave directions. Rebecca and Aaron thanked him and departed in haste. They found the streets of Flagstaff aswarm with a flurry of construction and commerce. All the snatches of conversation they overheard revolved around the army's latest move, something the poor colonel assumed to be secret. At the general mercantile, Rebecca and Aaron stopped to resupply their trail rations and obtain more ammunition.

"I say the army's in the wrong," a portly gentleman in a three-piece suit and derby hat brayed from his place by the post office window on one side of the general store. "Mac Kellogg is a captain of industry, a major factor in the success of this community. He's a sterling fellow, believe me. The damned army's supposed to protect us white folks from the stinkin' savages, not the other way around."

"Luke, you've got your head up your a—a—uh, pardon, ma'am," another local man blurted, blushing when he saw Rebecca enter. "You're wrong, anyhow. I've heard how that lumber got sold time and again, same boards, an' people are waitin' to take delivery. Kellogg's a crook."

"Who says?" Luke, the robust one, challenged.

"Not who, Luke—what. If Big Mac wasn't a crook, why would he have a horde of outlaw types working for him? Quiz me that one, eh?"

Neither Rebecca nor Aaron missed that reference. Taking a step closer to the disputing businessmen, Aaron questioned them while Rebecca placed their order for bacon, dry beans, and other essentials. "Gentlemen, you're talking about outlaws? If this Big Mac has hardcases working for him, are there any you know of who might be capable of murdering people to get them off their land?"

Luke rubbed vigorously at his chin with thumb and forefinger. His detractor took on an expression of eagerness. "I'll say there are. Half a dozen, at least. That John Duffey, for instance. He's got a shifty look, funny, beady eyes. He drinks like a fish. I wouldn't trust him around my bank any more than I'd put a fox in the henhouse to guard it."

"Dang it, Harry, you're just carryin' tales. Nothing in the world to prove what you implied," Luke protested. "Mister, I don't know what business it is of yours, but Harry here has a wild hair, is all. He's maligning one of the finest, most upstanding businessmen in our community."

"That so? Well, my business is the law. Deputy United States Marshal, Aaron Hawkins. Way I hear it, the army thinks Kellogg or some of his men are guilty of over twenty murders, in a Shoshone village. Might be my reason for being in town will put me on his trail, too."

Harry seized the opportunity. "There, you see? You see, Luke? The marshal here thinks Kellogg's a crook."

"I didn't say that. I only want to hear from folks about

183

any suspicious characters hanging around town that might have killed a few folks, including some prospectors. If talking to Kellogg will clear it up, then that's what I'll do."

The transactions completed, Rebecca nodded to Aaron and they departed. Twenty minutes later they were out of the Flagstaff basin and well on their way to where the army intended to encounter Kellogg's men.

"Sergeant, it's sure as hell these aren't any damned lumberjacks," Lieutenant Matthew Koenig remarked to his platoon sergeant.

The two soldiers hugged the ground behind a low rill that divided the open ground near the sawmill. Koenig had not even had time to do more than annouce the purpose of their unexpected visit before the fighting broke out. Men detailed to search the storage sheds came under fire from the tree line behind the lumber stacks. He'd ordered his command deployed, and those still mounted charged the unseen shooters. All hell broke loose on their left flank.

Another wave of heavily armed men rushed them on horseback. Mindful of the need for holding the high ground, Lieutenant Koenig had led his men to their present position. That had been twenty minutes ago. Since then the battle had degenerated to occasional sniping from both sides. Unfortunately for him, Matt Koenig admitted to himself, the enemy had the freedom to maneuver in any direction they wanted, except a direct frontal assault of the hillside.

"Another thing, sir. There's too fucking many of them," Sergeant Hammond remarked.

"And they fight like trained troops," Koenig added to their list of woes. "I don't think we'll be exaggerating to file in the report that we made contact with the force 'of unknown quantity' that attacked the Shoshones," he added dryly.

The sergeant chuckled. "No, sir. Not a bit. Only thing is, are we going to be around to file a report?"

"Losing hope, Sergeant Hammond?"

"Not at all, sir. Just making an observation. There's about twenty-five of the bastards moving through the trees over there. I don't see any sign of rifles, but they're carryin' gunny sacks."

"Meaning?"

"We could be in a hell of a lot of trouble, sir."

A rippling blast of three explosions in a row came a second later. Lieutenant Koenig's face went blank and he spoke in a shaky voice. "Jesus. That's dynamite, Sergeant. You were right. We're in a hell of a lot of trouble."

"Beggin' your pardon, sir, but the son-of-a-bitch running that bunch is a military genius."

"Quite right, I'm afraid. Now if he combines that improvised artillery with a cavalry charge, we'll know we've come up against a frontier Napoleon."

Sergeant Benson produced a rueful expression. "Sir, I'm thinkin' it's more likely us who've come upon our Waterloo."

Chapter 18

Constant use by lumber wagons plying back and forth to Big Mac Kellogg's timber camps had compacted the roadway into a wide, easily traversed thoroughfare. Rebecca Caldwell and Aaron Hawkins made excellent time northward from Flagstaff. By midafternoon they had come close enough to hear muted gunfire and the soft crump of explosives.

"Sounds like a regular war," Aaron opined.

"It's the next thing to it, I'd say. The point is, who's winning? That's not cannon fire, and the army doesn't use dynamite."

Aaron produced a quizzical expression. "Ever hear of hand grenades?"

"What are they?" Rebecca returned, unfamiliar with the term.

"Hand-thrown explosive charges. Like little cannon-balls, with the same, but smaller, effect when they blow up. They put out a regular shower of metal fragments moving fast enough to kill."

"That's . . . ghastly," Rebecca declared.

"Sure it is. But if I had a limited number of troops, with a large area to patrol and plenty of potential enemies, I'd requisition several cases and see that my men knew how to use them. They're very effective, and in one form or another, they've been around for several hundred years. That's where the term *grenadiers* comes from."

"You're just a fount of grisly information," Rebecca quipped.

"At least you can still laugh. D'you think Chris Starret might be mixed up in this?"

Surprised that Aaron hadn't brought up the subject of Starret for two days, Rebecca considered the possibility before answering. "We've heard nothing that would suggest it. Even so, I wouldn't be surprised if he was. One of the men in Flagstaff mentioned a name that's nagging me—John Duffey. Chris used to run with a man named Duffey. If this is the same one, Chris is likely to be here also."

"You're grabbing at straws again, Becky," Aaron advised lightly. "There's lots of Duffeys in the country. Also O'Brians, Brennans, O'Days, and other Irish surnames."

"I know—I know. It's . . . just a—a—ah, feeling I'm getting. Now don't laugh at this, it's sort of difficult to describe," Rebecca prefaced her explanation, acutely aware of the ridicule her "Indian ways" engendered in Gaylen Stanton. She slowed Śila to a walk. "Call it a premonition, maybe. I see it as images and shapes. Among the Sioux, I'd call it a vision or a medicine dream." She laughed uneasily. "Only I'm wide awake and riding beside you. This John Duffey seems to be the key, all right. And through him, I think we'll find Chris Starret."

Aaron coughed discreetly. "I, ah, think I know what you mean. I used to have that sort of thing happen when I was a kid. I also knew what some people were thinking, before they said anything. At least I did until my parents told me often enough that such things were impossible."

Unsettling to Aaron, Rebecca let go a trill of relieved chuckles. "Oh, Aaron, that's wonderful. I often thought I was somehow different, not really a human in the sense of how other people acted. Then, when I found out I was half Sioux, I believed it was because of my Indian blood. It's a relief to find out others have experienced the same sort of thing."

Aaron blushed, grinning, as he answered. "Ah—there's something I neglected to tell you. I said I came from Kansas, which is true. But from that part of the state that used to be in the Nations before statehood. My grandmother on my mother's side was three-quarter Osage."

Merriment rippled out of Rebecca's entire being. "Oh, Aaron, maybe it is just us with Indian ancestors. I found an answer that's no answer at all." Suddenly she sobered. "If we push it, we can catch up to that battle in less than an hour."

"I'm for that," Aaron agreed.

Chris Starret looked across the open ground to where the soldiers had taken defensive positions among the rocks and trees. One massed attack should sweep them out of there and send the survivors scurrying for Flagstaff. Damn it, how could this have happened? Big Mac had been right. The army was supposed to protect white settlers, not arrest them. What crime had they committed? They'd only killed a few Indians. He spat on the ground and turned to John Duffey.

"Blackjack, we're going to run those blue-bellies out of there. Get the men mounted up."

"This don't make much sense," Duffey responded, echoing Starret's own doubts. "Picking a quarrel with the army can only bring more army down on us."

Chris spoke confidentially. "You and I won't be here to see that. We're going to take what we've got and leave."

"When?"

"A week. More likely less than that. We'll stop off in Phoenix, skim the rest of the cream off my marks, and then head for San Francisco. Now let's get the men organized for a charge. Uh-oh, it looks like they're doing something over there."

"We going to attack anyway?" Duffey asked.

"We'll see what they're fixing to do first," Chris decided.

"*Boots and Saddles,* Sergeant," Lieutenant Koenig announced. "You'll lead the main body, and I'll take the charge of the rear guard."

"Pardon, sir, but hadn't that ought to be my job?" Sergeant Hammond asked seriously.

"I know, Sergeant. But I have this theory about leadership. The men left behind to hold off the enemy will be a lot more steady if they see me here with them. It's remarkable how such gestures can inspire men to fight like demons. Now, every man leaving is to surrender half of his remaining ammunition to those staying behind."

"Already done, sir. We, ah, can head out any time."

"Then make it so, Sergeant. And . . . good luck."

"More luck to you, sir. I'll see you at the post, sir."

"That's something we can both hope for. We'll open fire to cover your withdrawal."

Sudden and loud, a crashing volley of fire came from beyond the brow of the saddleback ridge toward which Rebecca and Aaron rode at a fast canter. Another disciplined volley roared out, followed by the firecracker rattle of men firing at targets of opportunity. Heavier here, the detonation of explosives answered the riflery.

"Something's changed," Rebecca shouted over the noise.

"And not for the good," Aaron added, pointing ahead to where a ragged column of blue-coated men galloped over the ridge. "This I don't believe. A bunch of gunslicks routing the army?"

190

"Not if I'm right. I've learned a lot about Chris Starret, in trying to track him down. He was an officer, a field commission, in the Union Army for the last years of the war. I can well imagine that John Duffey served at one time or another."

Aaron anticipated her. "Together they could put together a trained force capable of defeating troops unaccustomed to combat. Is that what you mean?"

"Exactly. Now I think we had better make some sign of peaceful intent. Rattled as those boys are, we might get shot by accident," Rebecca advised.

Aaron rigged an off-white shirt from his saddlebag to the barrel of his rifle and waved it above his head. Slowing slightly, the troops continued in their direction. When the fleeing column converged with them, the sergeant at the head of the soldiers touched his hatbrim in respect.

"Pardon me, folks, but you're headed into one hell of a mess over there."

"What is it, Sergeant?" Aaron asked.

"Might be I could tell you more if I knew who you are," Sergeant Hammond prompted.

After the introductions, Aaron asked his question again. Sergeant Hammond answered in detail, concluding with a bitter remark. "Must be near a hundred of 'em. They've got good leadership, which is strange for that type; fight like troops, too. We were no match for their tactics. If I had some of those boys that're fighting down south with Crook, I could have rolled 'em up right quick."

"They sent you out here in command of inexperienced men?" Aaron asked.

"Nope. The lieutenant's over th' other side with the rear guard. His idea. A good one, too. The men think the world of him now."

"When is he going to break off the engagement?" Rebecca asked.

"Soon's we have time to gain a few miles' advantage."

His worried expression changed to a retributive scowl. "We'll be coming back, you can bet on that. We'll bring that six-pounder at the outpost along, too. That'll cut off their water sure enough. I suppose that's it, folks. We'd best be riding."

"Another gun doesn't amount to much, but I think I'll join your rear guard," Aaron volunteered.

"Two guns," Rebecca said in a tone that prevented objection.

"You're both crazy," Sergeant Hammond opined.

"We've done enough here," Lieutenant Koenig informed Corporal Lang. "Send six men ahead to establish an ambush point, then we'll pull out five minutes later. By leap-frogging we can hold them back a goodly distance."

"Yes, sir. I'll send Johnson, Lowery and . . ." Corporal Lang named his "volunteers."

Massed fire had blunted the charge of the gunmen. They had broken into two wings that turned aside and rode back to the cover of buildings and trees. Matthew Koenig waited tensely for the minutes to tick off, then gave the order to mount. He led his men cross country to join the main road at an angle beyond the ridge. His surprise showed clearly on his face when two civilians came into view, one of them waving some sort of white flag.

"We're here to give what help we can," Aaron informed the harried officer. "Met up with your six men and they said to tell you the ambush will be around that bend at the river ford."

"Good place," Koenig acknowledged. "We'll ride there at once."

"I'd make it quick, sir," Lang offered. "Jones is high-tailin' it over the ridge. That bunch of gunhawks must be on their way."

Shallow, with not too rapid a current, the ford of the

Little Colorado proved an excellent ambush site. The first six of Chris Starret's men to round the bend died in a hail of lead. Three more received wounds from the second volley. That scattered the outlaw band, sent them back up the trail a quarter mile to rethink their approach.

"All right, we'll hold here," Koenig announced. "Six men again, Corporal, to establish the next ambush."

"Right away, sir."

Lang sent his men off and returned to the hastily made breastworks of driftwood and damp earth. No matter that scant minutes went by, the time seemed to drag maddeningly. A rumble of horses' hoofs broke the monotony of waiting.

"Here they come," Koenig warned.

Rebecca took aim on an imaginary spot near the bend. The buckhorn rear sight of her Winchester Express dissolved into a mere sensed presence as she concentrated on bringing the front post instantly into line with the first human target she saw.

"Hold your fire now . . . hold your fire," Koenig chanted. "Ready . . . here they come . . . aim . . . *fire!*"

Flame spurted from eighteen muzzles, and the lead two riders literally flew from their saddles, slammed by six bullets each. The men behind them spread out, jumped their horses into the water. One such hapless outlaw found a deep pool into which he and his horse sank from sight. In brief, gunshot-punctuated seconds the panicked animal surfaced, whinnied wildly, and thrashed to gain purchase. The rider's body washed up on the pebbles of the ford.

"Ready . . . aim . . . *fire!*" Lieutenant Koenig bellowed again. "Aim . . . *fire!* Now, Corporal."

Corporal Lang stood and shouted over the tumult, "Horse soldiers forward. Prepare to mount . . . *mount.*"

In seconds they whirled away and rode down the wide trail toward distant Flagstaff. So far they had gained maybe twenty minutes for the main detachment. Silently Koenig hoped Sergeant Hammond had thought of setting up an ambush of his own.

Chris Starret sat his horse in the saddleback notch of the ridge. Beside him, John Duffey swore at the distant sound of well-controlled volleys.

"Why didn't we go in there with our own boys, Chris? We could have wiped out that blue-belly rear guard."

"At what cost, Blackjack? Let our new recruits get a taste of battle. They and Big Mac's lumberjacks can serve as cannon fodder. The more of them who are killed or captured and identified, the harder it will be to trace any of this to you and I. We'll take the best of our lot with us when we pull out, and never worry about Kellogg again."

"Damn it," Lieutenant Matthew Koenig cursed hotly. "Three ambushes before those bastards broke contact. They're good, damned good. I wish I had them in uniform to fight for us."

Rebecca Caldwell studied the young officer, already impressed by his coolness under fire. He had a right to be bitter, she acknowledged. But she sensed something else lying right below the surface. Was it disillusionment?

"For certain sure they had one hell of a field commander," Koenig went on.

"Lieutenant, did you happen to see a certain man among them? Tall, slender, broad shoulders and completely bald?"

"Of course," Koenig responded. "He was leading them. That's Mac Kellogg's new partner, Chris Starret."

"I knew it," Rebecca all but shouted. "See, Aaron. Chris is behind all this. Attack the Shoshone? Of course. Fight the army? Only Chris would have nerve enough to do that." Quickly she explained her outburst to Lieutenant Koenig and convinced him she knew a considerable amount about Christopher Starret.

"Would you two be willing to sign on as contract

scouts?" Koenig requested.

"You've got my services no matter what," Aaron reminded him. "Comes with the Marshal's badge. And for that matter, now we know for sure it's Chris Starret, I've come to believe the killings I came here to investigate were done by him, or at his bidding. Which means if I don't stick with you, with the army, then I don't get a crack at him."

"I'll be glad to," Rebecca said eagerly.

Another potential problem goaded Lieutenant Koenig. "What about the Indians? Will they be mixing in, maybe become a hindrance to our rounding up Starret?"

"I think I've already set in motion something to take care of that possibility," Rebecca informed him.

"What's that?"

"Before leaving Denver, I sent a telegram to Lieutenant Arthur Trapp in Wyoming to get word to Chief Shining Horse that I would look into the trouble about which the Chief contacted me through Trapp."

"Somehow I get the feeling I'm missing out on something," Koenig said ruefully. "What exactly is your interest?"

"I've already explained this to Lieutenant Colonel Alford," Rebecca replied, then repeated her part in the events, revealing as little as she could. "So," she concluded, "I think I'll go on with my original plan. I'll go see the local Shoshone and work out something to keep them at peace while you deal with Chris Starret."

"It would be a miracle if you pull it off. Though I'm worried you have a lot more—ah—intestinal fortitude than you do good sense. The Shoshone are powerful mean, right about now."

Rebecca shrugged, then wrinkled her nose. "I'll have to take my chances. And alone," she added for Aaron's benefit.

Chapter 19

Rich laughter, hoots, and hollers drowned out birdsong at the sawmill. They had beaten the army. Run them the hell out of the country. In spite of his earlier determination that it would be necessary to make a quick escape to avoid ultimate retribution, Chris Starret rode high as any of the jubilant men celebrating their victory. Only Big Mac Kellogg didn't see it that way. Nor did Lupe Bargas.

Big Mac had just been told that the best bull cook he had ever had in camp wanted to quit. "I theenk maybe the so'jers come back. They bring plenty men, like the Federales in Mexico, an' keel us all. I didn' do any of the keeling of *los indios*, and I don' see why I should be punish' like all those who did. So I take my pay and say *adios*."

Mac paid him off and relayed all that to Chris, concluding, "What if they *do* bring more soldiers?"

Deeming it necessary to keep Big Mac calm and in peace to act as a diversion for his own escape, Chris sought to allay the burly lumberman's worries. "From where? Crook is busy along the border with the Apaches. You told me that junior grade colonel told you so. So that means there are no troops to spare."

"You didn't wipe them out, you know. The ones at Flagstaff, I mean," Mac countered. "And they didn't send all of them here. There's at least another platoon. We could have gone along, toughed it out, hired a good lawyer. No white jury is going to condemn men who killed some Indians."

"I prefer not to take chances with juries." Chris spoke hotly, from past experience. "Speaking of killing Indians, now is the time to wipe out the Shoshone and get on with the logging."

"Are you mad? With the army nipping at us, and a third of my men dead or wounded?"

"We'll take care of the Indians. You just keep cutting trees." Chris refrained from telling Mac that he had an accomplice on his way back East to line up suckers to put deposits on parcels of the land being stripped of its forest.

"I think you're making a mistake. A really big mistake. Look, we can blame the shootout with the army on the dead men, say they took it on themselves. If we patch it up with Colonel Alford, we can go on harvesting trees, cut all the lumber we can and be gone from here long before any trial can begin. But let the army stay pissed at us and who knows what they'll do."

"Damn little. What about the Shoshone?" Chris pressed.

"It's against my better judgment. Still, it keeps you and your private army out of sight and away from any other incident with the soldiers. Go on. If you can stop them from boozing, maybe you can be out of here yet today."

With the helpful information from Lieutenant Koenig, Rebecca left the army column at once. She took time only to change into her Sioux clothing, then headed for the area described as being the new summer camp for the Shoshone. Well before sundown she encountered a small hunting party. Using sign language she made her peaceful intentions clear to them and rode back to the village in their company. Her arrival heralded by the camp crier, she rode into the village to the silent, hostile looks of the residents.

Not even the usual flock of yelling children paraded behind her. When the hunt leader halted before a large lodge, obviously that of the chief, she waited quietly and did not dismount until the men had. Summoned by the words of the hunters, Walks Around came out of his lodge, bending low to allow his feathered war regalia to pass through the opening.

"Do any of you speak Lakota?" Rebecca asked in that language.

Blank-faced and unspeaking, a dozen men faced her now, the council, she supposed, and others in influence. When the quiet became strained, one young man stepped forward.

"I am Victor Cutshair," he said in English. "Do you speak English?"

Relieved, Rebecca allowed a small flicker of smile. "Yes, I do. Tell your chief that I am known as White Robe Woman of the Red Top Lodges Oglala."

When that had been conveyed, a noticeable thaw in attitudes spread among those who came to examine her. Walks Around spoke in his own language.

"Our chief, Walks Around, says to make you welcome. He has heard of you from Shining Horse, chief in the north. You will eat with us and then talk with the council." Walks Around spoke again. "The chief wants to know if you have brought warriors to help fight the evil whites."

Rebecca pursed her lips. "No. I have come alone. I want to speak of peace."

"*Wagh!* There can be no peace, until the white eyes are dead," Victor snarled.

"That needn't be done, the army is willing to help you maintain peace," Rebecca insisted. "Last year I made peace between the Shoshone and the Arapaho. If I can do

199

that, at least listen to what I say and decide then."

"You will be feasted. Then the council will meet."

"Good," Rebecca gusted out, relieved not to have failed. At least, so far.

Aaron accompanied the troops back to Flagstaff. They arrived late that night. Even so the town remained in full operation. Music tinkled from saloons, where the deep, hearty laughter of men and the high voices of women drifted into the streets invitingly. The odor of beer and whiskey teased Aaron's nostrils. More demanding were the rumbles set up by his stomach when they passed an eating house: the fragrance of frying porkchops and onions painfully reminded the lawman that he had not eaten since that morning. He excused himself to Lieutenant Koenig, promising to come to the cantonment and give his comments to Lieutenant Colonel Alford after he had eaten.

In the café, Aaron crowded onto a stool at the counter and looked anxiously for a waitress. Talk among the patrons centered on the army's ignominious return to Flagstaff in defeat. Most seemed to favor that situation. When one tippler, trying to recover sobriety through a plateful of fried potatoes, eggs, and a slab of ham, reminded everyone that the soldiers had started out to arrest some of Big Mac's loggers, another wag declared that they had gotten what they deserved.

"It weren't *them* whupped the soldier boys," an old man with a two-day salt-and-pepper stubble on his lean jaw contradicted. "Way I figger it, they never got to Mac's place. It was them Injuns did it. You know the way those Shoshone have been riled of late? Musta seen the soldiers comin' into their hunting grounds and figgered they were there to finish what some other fellers started. So they whupped 'em good."

"What d'you know, Axel? You got an Old Forester

bottle for brains."

Axel blinked owlishly and belched a gust of bourbon fumes. "I may be a drunk, Tandy Hanks, but I know what I know. Them boys had the green tinge comes from fightin' savages. Scared plum to death they was. I'm willin' to bet a prime bottle of Overholt's Rye that come tomorrow mornin', we'll be hearin' how the soldier-boys run afoul of the Shoshone. Or the Ute. Or it might of been the Navajo. One of them heathen tribes, anyhow."

A rat-faced individual who had entered during Axel's boozy ramble walked to the center of the room, right beside Aaron's place. "Then I say this. It's dirty work got done to our soldiers. What every one of us should do is volunteer to go out there and make the murderin' redskins pay."

"Right!" "You're right about that," came quick shouts of agreement. "How we gonna do that? D'you see what they did to those soldiers?"

Affecting a secretive expression and superior smirk, the man's thin lips parted, revealing over-large front teeth that enhanced his rodentlike appearance. "I happen to know some fellows who'd be mighty pleased to get some extra guns on their side. Fellows who have already made Mr. Lo pay for some of his evil. Any of you boys want to join up and help clean out this red scum, you come see me in the Orient Saloon right after you finish eatin'."

Conversation broke into independent groupings, and Aaron lost the main drift of opinion. He kept in mind what the ferret-faced agitator had said, particularly in light of what they had learned from Lieutenant Colonel Alford and Lieutenant Koenig. When his meal came and he'd assuaged the pain in his protesting innards, Aaron departed for the saloon. He found the man he wantd seated at a small table in an out-of-the-way corner.

"Howdy," Aaron greeted as he came up to the rat-faced man. "I heard your little speech in the cafe.

M'name's Aaron."

"They call me Benjie," came from behind the big, yellowed teeth. "You reckon to join up?"

"Maybe. First, I'd like to ask you a few questions about these men you know who have been making the Injuns pay lately." As he spoke, Aaron thumbed back the left lapel of his coat, revealing the U.S. Marshal's badge.

Although seated, Benjie managed an astonishing leap backward, upsetting his chair with a loud crash and scattering patrons at the next table. While he still backpedaled on empty air, his hand went to his waist and he whipped out a short-barrel .45 Colt Peacemaker. Fast as his reputation in other parts claimed, Benjie hadn't enough steam to beat Aaron Hawkins.

Aaron's full-barrel Colt came into his hand in a blur, the long, blued steel flashing in the lamplight. He had the hammer back as the front sight cleared leather and when his elbow whipped inward against his ribcage, Aaron's trigger finger dropped onto the thin spur of metal. The sear tripped and the hammer fell while Benjie still tried to align his weapon, his mouth drawn into a round "O."

Yellow-orange flame lanced from Aaron's six-gun. That close to his target, the burning gasses set Benjie's shirt front afire. The bullet punched through the rodent-faced hardcase before he knew he had been killed. His body slammed to the floor in a shower of sawdust, and his revolver went off. The bullet scarred the floorboards. Aaron stood over him, smoking Colt in his hand. Benjie blinked once . . . twice, and sighed heavily as though the weight of the whole world rested on his stomach.

"I reckon you done killed me," he panted. His face twitched from the pain, as beads of oily sweat popped out on his forehead. "T-tell Chris I'll meet him in hell."

"Shit!" Aaron exploded in the instant after Benjie died. "I sure messed up that lead." He turned then, conscious of a deadly silence in the room. "It's all right, folks. I'm the U. S. Marshal. This man drew on me first."

Aaron exposed his badge and watched the play of emotions on the bar patrons' faces. Some of them seemed as disgusted as he was. Losing a chance to interrogate one of Chris Starret's men sure made his day.

Hunting had been good, and the feasting lasted a long while, with a wide variety of foods. Much was made of the Sioux warrior woman. Rebecca, in turn, enjoyed the easy hospitality of the Shoshone. After the dances at the end of the meal, including one in which live rattlesnakes were used, the council adjourned to Walks Around's lodge. After the usual preliminaries, and a long oration by the civil chief, Rebecca was asked to make her contribution.

Uncertain of how to proceed, she began by recounting what she had accomplished the previous year in the dispute between their northern cousins and the Arapaho. She also pointed out the role Chris Starret had played in that dangerous situation. Then she asked what had been done so far, if anything, to obtain help from the government.

"We talked with the soldier-chief in the new place of whites," Walks Around explained. "He tells us that he can do nothing. Many of this council believe that it is only their usual way. The soldiers protect the whites while they destroy us."

"I talked with Lieutenant Colonel Alford. He seemed most distressed that he could not help you. He assured me that he had no choice in the matter . . . not enough troops."

"Our agent wrote words for us on paper. They tell of the evil things done," Moon Rider informed Rebecca. "These go to the big village of Wash-ing-ton. Also to the soldier-chief. But nothing is done to help us."

"White men come and burn our village," another member of the council began, describing the attack that had forced them to move so recently.

"The soldiers were sent to punish the white men who did that," Rebecca answered. For the present, she didn't want to bring up the fact of the army's defeat. "They now fight on your side. Do not take to the warpath again until they have a chance to punish the evildoers."

"It is a bad thing," Red Shirt stated flatly.

Which last sentiment, in varying forms, occupied the rest of the evening. Early in the morning, Rebecca was awakened by a girl in the last of her pre-teen years. By signs she indicated Rebecca was to follow her. She took the white squaw to a place along the stream and indicated where the women washed. Then she departed to leave Rebecca alone for her ablutions. When Rebecca returned to the lodge of her appointed host and hostess, she felt well rested and refreshed. After breakfast, the council reconvened. Something new had been added, or perhaps learned, Rebecca surmised when she saw the solemn faces of the council members.

"We have heard of a fight between the soldiers and the evil ones who attacked our village. The soldiers were beaten and driven off, is that so?"

Nothing for it now, Rebecca decided. Her reluctance had to be put aside. "Yes. The soldier-chief, Alford, sent out young men with no experience at war. The outlaws . . ." How did she explain that one? "who fought them had a good leader, the same one who caused trouble for your cousins to the north. They fought well and the soldiers had to turn away."

"That is all they will do?" Moon Rider asked in consternation. "Are the soldiers craven dogs that will show their bellies in submission?"

"Not at all. They will fight again. Now they have tasted fighting and are angry in their defeat. They will want revenge."

"How can you be sure, daughter of the Sioux?" Walks Around demanded.

"I . . . just am. I was with them at the last of the battle.

Those men fought bravely. All of them spoke angrily of being shamed by criminals." Let the translator, Cutshair, worry over that one. "It would be a bad time for you to turn on all the whites. It would mean you broke your word. The soldiers have not broken theirs. They tried and will try again."

"Bold words," a dissenter grumbled. "How do we know this?"

Rebecca allowed a little anger to seep through. "Because I said so. I am an Oglala warrior woman, and I do not lie."

"You must excuse us some harsh words, *Sinaskawin*. It is a surprise to us that the soldiers fought our enemy," Walks Around soothed. "Their defeat must not let us lose sight of our purpose. We have lived at peace with the whites for a long time. Yet we cannot let these evil ones go unpunished. I am sending for men in camp you have not met. They come from other people than ours. All want to fight the white men. Tell them what you have told us, that we might prevent a war that will spell only disaster for all our people."

It took only ten minutes for the representatives of the Ute and Navajo people to arrive. They listened in hard-faced impatience to what Rebecca recounted. Several nodded at the wisdom of forbearance. Two remained openly hostile. Rebecca sought to cajole them and the Shoshone council into agreeing not to wantonly attack any whites they encountered.

Exhausted from her oratorical efforts, Rebecca did not relent on a single point. Late in the afternoon, hunger more than persuasive disruption brought a suggestion of dismissing the council until the next day. Rebecca felt a warm gratitude for Moon Rider's recommendation. She yielded for one of the allies to express his opinion and sat down for the first time in two hours. Excited voices began to grow in volume and number outside. Walks Around signaled one of the doorkeepers to look into it.

205

He returned in a state of agitation, with a slender youth in his early teens. "This boy says the camp crier sent him. White men have been seen around the rim of the basin. They are moving into positions to attack us. They are the same ones who came before, the men who defeated the army."

Consternation turned to anger, and excited yells for war ponies came from several councilmen. Rebecca's face reflected blank surprise, and she forced herself to think quickly. Turning to Walks-Around, she captured his attention.

"I must get my belongings," she pleaded. "Get my guns. I will fight with you."

Chapter 20

Two owls kept up a chatty *too-whoo* conversation in tall pines outside the low palisades of the army outpost in Flagstaff. Ten minutes after he shot Benjie, Aaron Hawkins walked through the gate. He informed the sentry that he needed to see Lieutenant Colonel Alford and Lieutenant Koenig. He was escorted to the head-quarters orderly room and asked to wait.

"Ah, there you are," Lieutenant Koenig greeted, coming in the door, one hand busy closing the last two buttons on his tunic. "Bit late for making your statement, isn't it?"

"Yeah. Something got in the way."

"Is this the young man who so gallantly volunteered his aid, Matt?"

Lieutenant Colonel Alford bustled into the orderly room and extended a hand. Aaron shook it and tried to force a self-deprecating smile. He felt his actions had been born of duty and was distinctly uncomfortable with praise.

"Yes, it is, sir. I gather he's come to make his statement," Koenig responded.

"Hmm. I didn't expect you until tomorrow when you didn't show up right after we had late chow."

"I was explaining to the lieutenant, I ran into a little problem. I just shot a man in the Orient Saloon. He

207

was recruiting anyone he could to fight Indians. I'm certain he worked for Chris Starret. The Shoshone got into the conversation a moment before I tried to arrest him. And before he died, he said to tell Chris he'd meet him in hell."

Alford produced a grimace. "I suppose that's all you got out of him?"

"I know, damn it, I'm not happy about it either. He could have told us a lot. I'm still convinced that Chris Starret intends to attack the Shoshone village again. After defeating the army—er—forced a strategic withdrawal, he's no doubt riding high. It's consistent with his past behavior."

"The question is, when?" Alford mused aloud. "How much time do we have?"

"*That's* why I would like to have kept him alive. It could be any time, even now. Within the next few days for certain. This Benjie was pushing rather hard to get recruits."

"How soon can we get troops into the field, Matt?" the colonel asked.

"My men are dead tired, sir," Koenig reminded him.

"I'm aware of that. What I mean is, if we start now, can we have an effective force ready by first light tomorrow?"

"Yes, sir. That still leaves us with a platoon against nearly a hundred men, sir," Koenig prompted.

"There are two patrols that should be within a few hours' ride of here. We also have that artillery squad and the six-pounder. If need be, we can turn out these garrison rats and make soldiers out of them, too."

Koenig brightened. "That'll give us near equal strength, and the advantage of the field piece."

"Is there any way we can get a warning to the Shoshone?" Lieutenant Colonel Alford asked.

"If I can get two hours' sleep, I'll start right after that," Aaron offered.

"We'll need you with the column, Hawkins. You're

the only one who knows the way to that new campsite."

"Whatever you say, Colonel. Only, Rebecca's out there with the Indians. If Starret attacks, who knows what they'll do?"

Unaware of the Shoshones' reinforcement by allies, Chris Starret led his men in a wide frontal attack down the slope of the basin. The tactic had worked well before. Chivington had used it at Sand Creek against the Arapaho, Custer at the Washita against Black Kettle's Cheyenne, Colonel Ronald McKinzie did it that way in Palo Duro Canyon against the Kiowa and Cheyenne, and he had employed it three times with great success.

This time one critical factor would be missing. The village did not contain only women, children, and the sick and aged. Over two hundred warriors—Shoshone, Ute, and Navajo—waited for Chris. And one extremely worried half Sioux, Rebecca Caldwell. At the head of a force of ninety-seven, Chris Starret soon discovered his error.

Mobility and superior firepower are all that saved the self-styled Indian fighters from disaster. Although outgunned, the Indians relied on their traditional weapons. A cloud of arrows rose to greet the charging whites. Flint and metal arrowheads bit into flesh at random. Here a horse whinnied shrilly in pain and stumbled, there a man clutched an arm. A short distance away, another horse went down instantly, half of a feathered shaft protruding from its forehead. The abruptly disorganized whites managed two ragged vollies before they wheeled and dashed out of range.

"Get some rifles over here," Rebecca Caldwell shouted in the confusion caused by the initial assault.

"Our warriors fight with their own," the Navajo war chief stated flatly.

"Then they can die with their own," Rebecca snapped. At least he speaks English, she thought as she continued,

"These men fight like the pony-soldiers. If we don't have an organized defense, we might as well sit down and wait for them to come in and kill us." Inspiration struck her, and she raised her Express rifle and blew an outlaw out of his saddle.

"*That's* what we need more of. He was out of bowshot. If all the men with rifles in camp came over here, we could force them farther back and organize a counter-attack."

Listening from close by, Victor Cutshair translated for Walks Around. The old chief brightened and uttered a grunt. He went over to the Navajo Chief and placed a hand on the obdurate man's shoulder.

"White Robe Woman speaks wisely," he said in the Navajo tongue. "We can force them into the trees that way, then attack on their flank with half of all our fighting men. They do not number that many."

The squat, muscular Navajo thought on it a moment. "We will do this." He turned to a youth at his side. "Silver Horn, run and tell our warriors with guns to come over here."

After the boy sped away, he turned to Walks Around. "Will the ugly ones come as well?"

A thin smile formed on Walks Around's face. The Navajo people had no love for the Ute. "I will see it done."

Although maintaining a note of condescension, the Navajo chief turned to Rebecca. "How would you make this attack on their weak point?"

Relieved and elated, Rebecca Caldwell quickly began to lay out a plan for a counterattack.

After a routine departure from Flagstaff, the large body of troops began a forced march pace. The additional patrols would meet with them on the trail northward. Aaron found he had benefited from the night of sleep. Although saddle weary, he could keep up with the continuous routine of twenty minutes of canter, twenty at the walk, and the same leading their mounts. "Forty miles a day on beans and hay," the old song went. At this clip they could make seventy, he estimated.

"Koenig," he asked as they walked side-by-side at the head of the column, leading their mounts. "Doesn't the fast pace shake hell out of that cannon?"

"It would if it was still on its carriage. The tube's lashed on a pack mule. The artillerymen will put it back together when we get there."

"That won't be too soon for me. I keep thinking what might happen."

"Yeah. She's a beautiful woman. I only had her acquaintance for a few hours, and a lot of that fighting. Still, I can't help thinking how much I'd like it to be longer."

"I only hope there'll be a longer," Aaron confessed glumly.

Chris Starret mopped his powder-grimed face. Midday heat made their every movement an effort. He had led several charges, all of which had been turned back. The last most disastrously.

"Goddamn, they've got all their rifles on one side," he complained aloud to John Duffey. "Indians don't fight that way. None of them have chased after us, either. I wonder why?"

"Maybe they've got them an Indian that's soldiered down there," Duffey suggested.

"I doubt that. If they had someone capable of it, he'd have done his stuff the last time."

"Then how are they managing? They're not all Shoshone, you know."

"I saw that. Navajo, I'd judge from the long shirts with puffy sleeves and the trousers. Only why would they be fighting with an old enemy?"

"It's something we should know, only we don't. We'll

211

try one more go at it. If we can break their line, get inside the village, we can use fire on them."

"Good idea," Duffey allowed. "I'll go get the boys ready."

Red Shirt sat his favorite pony behind a fringe of closely spaced aspen. Their shimmering pale green leaves fluttered nervously in the steady light breeze that blew toward his hidden force of fifty men. He had listened to the words of the Sioux woman and wondered at the simplicity of such tactics. Why had they never used such a diversion before?

"Wait until the next charge. Then ride to the position you picked in those aspen."

"Then we fall upon them as they return?"

"No. When they attack again, and they will, you hit them from the side. The enemy will not be watching for you because they won't know you are on their flank."

It had worked out that way, too. While the whites rode at the village again, the picked men slipped away and circled wide to come into the forest on the north side. Now it looked like they would try another time to get into the village. Red Shirt's lips tightened. His wife and children were there. If the white-eyes began to burn lodges and shoot those fleeing the fires, their lives could be lost. Red Shirt forced himself to stop such thoughts. Yes. She had been right. The white-eyes would attack again.

Rifle fire greeted them halfway to the village. Undisciplined and poorly aimed for the most part, the flying lead presented only harassment. Chris Starret had a good feeling about this attack. Was it his imagination, or were there considerably less warriors standing them off? They'd learn soon enough.

Eerie whooping to his left brought Chris' attention in

that direction in time for him to see a charging band of warriors roll out of the trees. Coming from the side and slightly behind the attacking mass of his own men, the warriors had a distinct advantage. Already two horses ran wild, their saddles empty.

"Wheel left!" Chris bellowed. "They're on our flank. Forget the village. To the left, now!"

Cutting across the front, Chris waved his rifle to signal his men to follow him. He streaked toward the attacking Indians, intent this time on facing them with an effective force more than firing on them. A quick glance over his shoulder showed that the majority had reacted, although slowly. An arrow hummed its mournful tune past his ear, and he flinched away reflexively.

"Open fire," he commanded. "Cut 'em down."

Only a half dozen weapons fired before the two elements closed. Fierce hand-to-hand fighting broke out. The knife, tomahawk and lance had an advantage. The milling whites could not use their rifles except as clubs, nor their sidearms for fear of hitting each other. Chris saw a slender young brave in a red calico shirt and instinctively knew him to be the leader. He returned his rifle to its scabbard and drew a Smith & Wesson .44 Russian revolver.

He had time for only a single shot, Chris realized. The whirling melee eddied and turned on the slope. He took hurried aim and squeezed the trigger.

Almost at once his target reacted, jerking backward in his war saddle and clapping a hand to the narrow trough on top of his shoulder. Wincing, Red Shirt realized he had a broken collarbone. Chris cursed his lack of accuracy as the tumult spun him away from his view of the war leader.

It seemed only a minute more before the Indians broke through and rode shouting in triumph toward the village. "Damn them, goddamn them all," Chris swore blackly. "They'll not get away with that again. Fall back!"

Once more out of range of the deadly rifles, Chris

213

called a council of his most trusted men. "We're going to spread out, circle the village just out of range. We won't get caught by surprise again. That mess cost us eighteen men, mostly wounded, but five are dead. Every third man takes a saddlebag full of dynamite sticks and some fuse caps. We'll make sure none of them get out of there if they do try."

"Boss, c'mere a minute," Buck Rainey called from his observation post.

"What is it?" Chris asked as he walked to his henchman.

Rainey gestured with his binoculars. "Down there in the village . . . I think I found your military genius."

Chris took the field glasses and focused on the village. "Where?"

"Between those two lodges near the center. Someone talking with the old chief."

Chris located them. Finding the image in the eyepieces, he saw that Walks Around was indeed one of them. The other appeared to be a woman. She stood out from the others in a white beaded dress with long fringes. Her braids and the back of her head seemed familiar. It couldn't be, he rejected when he caught a fleeting flicker of her profile. Yet her costume, the decorative work, seemed out of place here. It wasn't Shoshone, definitely not Ute. She turned again, full face now. By God, it was her. How in hell had Rebecca Caldwell managed to show up here?

"You're right, Buck. That's her, the bitch. You remembered her from Wyoming last year, eh? No problem. She's only one woman, and we have her ass trapped. Help Blackjack get men positioned around the village. After dark they can slip in with their dynamite and finish this bunch of savages in no time."

After dismissing his council of war, Chris Starret went off in search of something to eat. Imagine, Rebecca Caldwell here, after all the misery he had made her endure. A gutsy lady. One he'd give anything to have on his side. Despite his easy assurances to Buck Rainey, he sure didn't like having her against him.

From their distance, the sound of sporadic firing could be heard. More like a sniper duel, Lieutenant Koenig assured Aaron, than anything else. Somehow the Indians must have managed a stand-off, Koenig helpfully suggested. Twenty minutes' ride and they should be in sight of the village.

"And none too soon," Aaron emphasized. "I've got a bad feeling about this."

"You don't think the Shoshone would do anything to her, do you?" Koenig asked, genuinely concerned.

"Who knows with Indians?" Aaron handed back. Then, stricken, his face washed blank, then twisted with agony. "*I* said that? And I'm in love with one."

Sympathy for his new friend directed Matthew Koenig's actions. "Sir," he addressed Alford. "Permission for Mr. Hawkins and myself to ride ahead and scout out the situation around the village, sir."

"Granted, Matt. Try to get a count on the attacking force. It appears they beat us here."

Matt Koenig and Aaron Hawkins rode off together at a faster pace than the column. Every soldier showed eagerness to even the score with the guerrilla army that had shamed them two days before. Aaron held no sympathy with the outlaws and riff-raff he had battled with the rear guard, yet he pitied anyone who had to face a rapid-firing cannon and a hundred and twenty-five angry troopers.

Chapter 21

Through the field glasses Matt Koenig had given him, Aaron Hawkins watched Chris Starret's men preparing three-stick bundles of dynamite. The sun lay low in the west, in perfect position to mask the approach of the troops, as Lieutenant Colonel Alford had planned it. Aaron took scant satisfaction in that, confronted with the murderous intent of the men below him. Like the young officer at his side, he made continuous sweeps of the outlaw positions.

He estimated nearly a hundred guns against the Indian village. In the cover of darkness they could bring on havoc with the explosives. So, too, could the army, he reminded himself. They had perhaps two hours before sunset. Even then the afterglow would provide light for another half hour. Plenty of time, if they got there soon enough.

"The troops are going to have quite a job on their hands," Matt whispered to Aaron.

"I know it. Any ideas how the colonel will handle it?"

Matt mused only a moment. "I'd say he'll set up for a charge, then have the six-pounder shell them a while and go in before they can recover."

"What about the Indians?" Aaron asked, concerned for Rebecca.

"If the cannon fire doesn't upset them too much, I'm

217

sure they'll manage to fight a little of this battle on their own," Matt spoke confidently. "Let's make one last sweep and head back."

Aaron did so and brief seconds later stiffened. A sharp grunt preceded a prolonged hiss of expelled air. "Look there, where the women are filling parfleches with dirt. In the white beaded dress. It's Becky. I'm sure of it."

Matt obligingly trained his glasses on the distant, tiny figures. "Ummm. Could be. Her back's to us, though."

"I want to wait until we're sure," Aaron demanded.

"We should have been studying the Indians as well," Matt observed a moment later. "Look, those men and boys are piling up lots of wood all around the village. You suppose they're going to light fires after dark?"

"Sure. If Starret orders an attack, his men will come out of the dark into bright light from those fires, they can't be more than thirty feet apart. The Shoshone on watch will be used to the brightness. And hidden behind those bags of dirt. It'll be a slaughter."

"You're forgetting the dynamite," Matt reminded him.

"Yeah. But not the six-pounder. Hit from behind by it, and trapped against a wall of fire and arrows, where can Starret's mob go? They won't have a chance." Less than a minute later, he started to rise. "We can go now. I saw her face. It's Becky."

It took Lieutenant Colonel Alford only two minutes to size up the situation and digest the report from Aaron and Matt. He issued precise orders and set junior officers and their noncoms to work carrying them out. When the report came up the chain of command that all men stood at their posts, he drew his saber and raised it high.

"Trumpeter, sound the charge."

Sweet, clear, and brassy, the notes of the charge sounded over the wide basin that sheltered the Shoshone encampment. Only two minutes before, Chris Starret's gunhawks had begun to move downward along the shadowed western slope. Once in motion, their minds riveted on the Indian force waiting them, they saw and heard nothing as the troops moved into position behind them. The sudden, crisp clarion froze them in place for a moment. Then they heard the flat double-thump of explosion and compressed air as the six-pound field piece fired its first round.

A shrieking whistle followed as the conical explosive projectile howled through the air. It struck among a dozen of the hired army. Men screamed in agony as hot shards of shrapnel lashed their bodies. Two died instantly just feet from the point of detonation. Another round warbled its song of death. There would be three fired before a minute passed. Mounted troopers, carbines at the ready, streamed from the woods to swarm down on the numb, demoralized riff-raff.

"Run fellers, it's the gawdamned army," one less-than-stout heart shouted.

"Lordy, I didn't sign on to fight a fuckin' cannon," another bleated as he threw down his rifle and began to race toward imagined safety to the north.

Six rounds banged out of the cannon before the point of aim changed to the northern slope. Vengeful troops charged in among Chris's guerrillas. Most of the hired-on civilians had already broken and ran pell-mell in terrified confusion. A handful of hardcore outlaws stood their ground and managed to maim a half dozen horses and men with their dynamite bombs. Still the soldiers pressed in on them. For a while the line of Starret's force dissolved into nothing. The end looked assured.

Then they stiffened their resistance and formed up to fight the soldiers to a standstill. A ragged cheer came from their ranks, to be answered by war whoops from the allied Indian bands. Ute, Navajo, and Shoshone came at them from behind. His mind set on one thing, Aaron Hawkins shot his way through the weak left flank of Starret's resistance and raced Buck toward the village.

Aaron didn't see the gunman who rose up out of the tall grass, his empty rifle held like a club. The man swung with considerable force and knocked the young marshal from the saddle. Winded and with blackness swimming before his eyes, Aaron looked up to see the man straddle him with a cocked six-gun pointed at his face. He rolled violently the instant the weapon discharged.

Hot pain exploded in his right shoulder. At least he had been spared for another moment. Acting quickly, the outlaw cocked his revolver again. Then he screamed as a Shoshone lance ripped into his back. Sagging, he fell over Aaron's supine body. Aaron waited until the warrior had satisfied himself of the other's death. The bronze skinned man started to walk away, then paused and looked directly into Aaron's eyes. He spoke in careful, precise English.

"I am called Victor Cutshair. I figured that anyone they wanted to hurt had to be on our side."

Groaning, Aaron extricated himself and thanked Victor. Then he started at a shambling walk into the village. Confusion made everyone anonymous. Already cooking fires burned, smoke from dripping fat making fog tendrils through the spaces between lodes. Aaron looked first where he had last seen Rebecca. She was not there. Why didn't he use his head? The women running for shelter from the growing battle all wore drab, brown dresses. Look for white. He did and found his search quickened. Near the crudely erected parapet, he saw a flash of white. Drawing on his fading reserves, Aaron forced himself into a halting run.

He reached the barricade, and Rebecca's side, a moment before the hopelessly outnumbered outlaw army made their final, mindless act of defiance. Dynamite bombs went off like a chain of giant firecrackers. Discharging weapons in every direction the crowded-in remnants of Chris Starret's army tried desperately to break free. Aaron joined Rebecca and several Shoshone when they climbed to the top of the embrasure to direct their weapons into the suicidal throng.

"Aaron," she said cheerily when she recognized him beside her.

Then she abruptly sat down. An expression of confusion changed to numbed pain and she grasped her right leg. "Ow. Oh, damn—damn it."

Bending, Rebecca pulled up the hem of her dress to reveal the blue, puckered lips of an entrance wound. The other side of her shapely calf bled profusely. "They shot you in the leg," Aaron blurted out the obvious.

"Yes, and now I can't go after Chris Starret. I saw him not two minutes ago. Right there in the middle of everything."

"He won't get away," Aaron said reassuringly.

Rebecca had to work hard to swallow back the tears that threatened to burn out of her eyes. "I'm—I'm not so sure of that. H-he's like the devil himself."

"I can't . . . I can't keep going," Chris Starret protested into the rapidly darkening sky near the rim of the basin above the Shoshone village.

"You've got to, Chris," John Duffey urged him. "Hell, those Injuns are gonna be out here collecting hair any time now. We'll do like you said, Chris. How about it? We go to Phoenix, get the money, then head out for San Francisco. I know that bullet hole hurts, but you've got to keep moving."

"Horses," Chris grunted. "We'll need horses to get away and—and I can't sit down to ride."

For all his urgency, John Duffey responded drolly. "I've never been shot in the ass before, Chris. How'd it happen?"

"Never mind, damn it," Chris growled. "You keep shut about that, and I'll make the effort to keep on walking. Somewhere we've got to find horses."

"And then?" Duffey prompted, worried that his long-time friend and partner in crime might lose heart and

221

give up.

For a tense, silent minute, Chris Starret stared up at the stars slowly fading into existence in the western sky. "San Francisco is lovely this time of year."

When the numbers got down to forty-nine, the first of the surviving guerrillas began to throw down arms and surrender. With a suddenness like its beginning, the battle came to an end. From among the captives, Rebecca picked out men she knew to have been followers of Chris Starret in times past. Lieutenant Koenig identified several he knew from the earlier battle. Some Ute brought in stragglers from the darkness. Then Red Shirt appeared with three prisoners. One Rebecca recognized as Buck Rainey.

"Where's Chris, Buck?" she asked him curtly, her temper frayed by pain and annoyance.

"I don't know. Lost sight of him in the fight . . . him and John Duffey."

"Are you lying to me?" Rebecca menaced.

"Why should I? I figure if I treat you square, you'll see to it these savages don't play any of their nasty little games with me."

"Where is the little boy Chris was holding captive? The Shoshone boy?" Rebecca asked, taking Buck off stride.

"Which one? There was two. One escaped."

"Don't be flip with me, or I'll personally stake you out over an ant hill."

Victor Cutshair stood close by, translating everything into his native tongue. Red Shirt listened closely, compelling concern for his missing son rekindled after the conflict ended.

"B'god I think you would," Rainey shuddered in answer. "He's dead. Chris wanted him questioned about this place. How to find it. Me an' the boys got a little too rough. I wound up wringing the little bastard's neck."

Buck Rainey's smirk clearly said, "What's so big about killing an Indian brat?"

He lost that snide expression a second later when Victor Cutshair completed his translation. Except for the tears that suddenly sprang from his eyes, Red Shirt betrayed none of the grief and rage he felt as he thrust forward with his lance and drove its broad, leaf-bladed point deep into Buck Rainey's belly. Buck shrieked and howled, then sagged to his knees, while Red Shirt slowly twisted the long blade in the smug outlaw's guts. When Rainey uttered a final whimper and his body convulsed in the release of death, Red Shirt gave the shaft a casual shake to dislodge the head and withdrew it.

"Take him away and burn him. Burn up everything so his spirit will forever wander in darkness," the grief-stricken warrior commanded.

A careful search by torchlight and another in early morning revealed no sign of Chris Starret or John Duffey. Rebecca sat and stared blankly into the sky, nursing the throbbing soreness in her calf.

"He got away again. And damn—damn—oh—damn, with this leg I can't go after him. He'll have money stashed somewhere. He has to go for that. If only I could ride."

"We'll find him," Aaron promised.

"We? What about your job, Aaron?"

"Chris Starret is my job. At least until he's caught and jailed, awaiting trial."

"Or killed," Rebecca amended. "After witnessing first hand the horrible things he does, or has done, surely you must feel a little like I do."

Aaron gave her a secretive smile. "I wouldn't want my superiors to hear me admit that. They'd take away my badge. Enough of Chris Starret for a while. We'd better get ready to leave."

"Why not stay here?"

"For now, we have to get you somewhere to have that wound treated."

"What about you? You have a hole in your shoulder."

"Maybe we can get the doc to treat two for the price of one."

"We can be treated right here, you know," Rebecca pointed out.

"I think I'd rather leave it up to a regular doctor. I don't want to take any chance of losing you."

"That's sweet. So we go in to Flagstaff. After the doctor, what did you have in mind?"

"I've been thinking about a large, soft, very strong bed, and a long, long recuperation for two."

Deep blue eyes sparkling, Rebecca clasped Aaron's cheeks in her warm, moist palms. "So, dear Aaron, have I."